BARRY GIFFORD'S
WILD AT HEART

"Barry Gifford is all the proof the world will ever need that a writer who listens with his heart is capable of telling anyone's story."
—Armistead Maupin, *San Francisco Chronicle*

"Gifford's book is a honey. It stuck to my fingers. *Wild at Heart* cuts right to the heart of what makes a good novel readable and entertaining: the voices of real people in it. The way Barry Gifford does it, it's high art."

—Elmore Leonard

"The story of Sailor and Lula is a purebred original. When the world finally takes its toll on these courageous lovers, we grieve both for them and for missed opportunities everywhere. Wild hearts often grow cold, but Sailor and Lula make us remember what it is to burn."

—*Booklist*

Books by Barry Gifford

Nonfiction

A Day at the Races: The Education of a Racetracker
The Devil Thumbs a Ride & Other Unforgettable Films
The Neighborhood of Baseball
Saroyan: A Biography (*with Lawrence Lee*)
Jack's Book: An Oral Biography of Jack Kerouac
  (*with Lawrence Lee*)

Fiction

Wild at Heart: The Story of Sailor and Lula
Port Tropique
Francis Goes to the Seashore
Landscape with Traveler: The Pillow Book of Francis Reeves
A Boy's Novel

Poetry

Ghosts No Horse Can Carry: Collected Poems 1967–1987
Giotto's Circle
Beautiful Phantoms: Selected Poems
Persimmons: Poems for Paintings
The Boy You Have Always Loved
Selected Poems of Francis Jammes (*translations, with Bettina Dickie*)
Coyote Tantras
The Blood of the Parade

WILD AT HEART

WILD AT HEART

THE STORY OF SAILOR AND LULA

BARRY GIFFORD

VINTAGE CONTEMPORARIES
VINTAGE BOOKS
A DIVISION OF RANDOM HOUSE, INC.
NEW YORK

*This book is dedicated
to the memory of
Charles Willeford*

"You need a man to go to hell with."

— *Tuesday Weld*

CONTENTS

CONTENTS

WILD AT HEART

GIRL TALK

LULA AND HER FRIEND Beany Thorn sat at a table in the Raindrop Club drinking rum Co-Colas while watching and listening to a white blues band called The Bleach Boys. The group segued smoothly from Elmore James's "Dust My Broom" into Robert Johnson's "Me and the Devil" and Beany let out a snort.

"I can't stand this singer," she said.

"He ain't so bad," said Lula. "Carries a tune."

"Not that, just he's so ugly. Guys with beards and beer guts ain't quite my type."

Lula giggled. "Seein's how you're about thick as a used string of unwaxed dental floss, don't know how you can criticize."

"Yeah, well, if he says all that flab turns into dick at midnight, he's a liar."

Lula and Beany laughed and swallowed some of their drinks.

"So Sailor's gettin' out soon, I hear," said Beany. "You gonna see him?"

Lula nodded and crushed an ice cube with her back teeth and chewed it.

"Meetin' him at the gate," she said.

"I didn't hate men so much," said Beany, "I'd feel better wishin' you luck."

"Can't all husbands be perfect," Lula said. "And Elmo

3

prob'ly wouldn'ta ever got that second one pregnant you hadn't kicked his ass out."

Beany twisted her blond bangs into a knot on her forehead.

"Shoulda put a thirty-eight long in his groin, what I shoulda done."

The Bleach Boys kicked into some kind of Professor Longhair swamp mambo and Beany grabbed a waitress.

"Bring us a couple more double-shot rum Co-Colas, 'kay?" she said. "Damn, Lula, look at that bitch wiggle."

"You mean the waitress?"

"Uh huh. Bet if I had a butt like hers Elmo wouldn'ta stuck his dick in every other keyhole this side of the Tangipahoa."

"Hard to say for sure," said Lula.

Beany's eyes watered up. "I guess," she said. "Only I'd give up plenty—Valiums even, maybe—just to have me some kind of a butt anyway, you know?"

WILD AT HEART

SAILOR AND LULA lay on the bed in the Cape Fear Hotel listening to the ceiling fan creak. From their window they could see the river as it entered the Atlantic Ocean and watch the fishing boats navigate the narrow channel. It was late June but there was a mild wind that kept them "not uncomfortable," as Lula liked to say.

Lula's mother, Marietta Pace Fortune, had forbidden her to see Sailor Ripley ever again, but Lula had no intention of following that order. After all, Lula reasoned, Sailor had paid his debt to society, if that's what it was. She couldn't really understand how going to prison for killing someone who had been trying to kill him could be considered payment of a debt to society.

Society, such as it was, thought Lula, was certainly no worse off with Bob Ray Lemon eliminated from it. In her mind, Sailor had performed a service beneficial in the short as well as the long run to mankind and should have received some greater reward than two years in the Pee Dee River work camp for second-degree manslaughter. Something like an all-expenses-paid trip for Sailor with the companion of his choice—Lula, of course—to New Orleans or Hilton Head for a couple of weeks. A top hotel and a rental car, like a snazzy new Chrysler LeBaron convertible. That would have made sense. Instead, poor Sailor has to clear brush from the side of the road, dodge

snakes and eat bad fried food for two years. Because
Sailor was a shade more sudden than that creep Bob Ray
Lemon he gets punished for it. The world is really wild at
heart and weird on top, Lula thought. Anyway, Sailor
was out now and he was still the best kisser she'd ever
known, and what Mrs. Marietta Pace Fortune didn't find
out about wasn't about to hurt her, was it?

"Speakin' of findin' out?" Lula said to Sailor. "Did I
write to you about my findin' Grandaddy's letters in the
attic bureau?"

Sailor sat up on his elbows. "Were we speakin'?" he
said. "And no."

Lula clucked her tongue twice. "I was thinkin' we'd
been but I been wrong before. Sometimes I get like that
now. I think somethin' and then later think I've said it out
loud to someone?"

"I really did miss your mind while I was out at Pee
Dee, honey," said Sailor. "The rest of you, too, of course.
But the way your head works is God's own private mys-
tery. Now what about some letters?"

Lula sat up and fixed a pillow behind her back. Her
long black hair, which she usually wore tied back and
partly wrapped like a racehorse's tail, fanned out behind
her on the powder blue pillowcase like a raven's wings.
Her large grey eyes fascinated Sailor. When he was on the
road gang he had thought about Lula's eyes, swum in
them as if they were great cool, grey lakes with small
violet islands in the middle. They kept him sane.

"I always wondered about my grandaddy. About why
Mama never chose to speak about her daddy? All I ever
knew was that he was livin' with his mama when he
died."

"My daddy was livin' with his mama when he died,"
said Sailor. "Did you know that?"

Lula shook her head. "I surely did not," she said. "What were the circumstances?"

"He was broke, as usual," Sailor said. "My mama was already dead by then from the lung cancer."

"What brand did she smoke?" asked Lula.

"Camels. Same as me."

Lula half rolled her big grey eyes. "My mama smokes Marlboros now," she said. "Used to be she smoked Kools? I stole 'em from her beginnin' in about sixth grade. When I got old enough to buy my own I bought those. Now I've just about settled on Mores, as you probably noticed? They're longer."

"My daddy was lookin' for work and got run over by a gravel truck on the Dixie Guano Road off Seventy-four," said Sailor. "Cops said he was drunk—daddy, not the truck driver—but I figure they just wanted to bury the case. I was fourteen at the time."

"Gee, Sailor, I'm sorry, honey. I never would have guessed it."

"It's okay. I hardly used to see him anyway. I didn't have much parental guiding. The public defender kept sayin' that at my parole hearin'."

"Well, anyway," said Lula, "turns out my mama's daddy embezzled some money from the bank he was clerkin' in? And got caught. He did it to help out his brother who had TB and was a wreck and couldn't work. Grandaddy got four years in Statesville and his brother died. He wrote Grandmama a letter almost every day, tellin' her how much he loved her? But she divorced him while he was in the pen and never talked about him to anyone again. She just refused to suffer his name. But she kept all his letters! Can you believe it? I read every one of 'em, and I tell you that man loved that woman. It must have broke him apart when she refused to stand by him.

7

Once a Pace woman makes up her mind there's no discussin' it."

Sailor lit a Camel and handed it to Lula. She took it, inhaled hard, blew the smoke out and half rolled her eyes again.

"I'd stand by you, Sailor," Lula said. "If you were an embezzler."

"Hell, peanut," Sailor said, "you stuck with me after I'd planted Bob Ray Lemon. A man can't ask for more than that."

Lula pulled Sailor over to her and kissed him soft on the mouth. "You move me, Sailor, you really do," she said. "You mark me the deepest."

Sailor pulled down the sheet, exposing Lula's breasts. "You're perfect for me, too," he said.

"You remind me of my daddy, you know?" said Lula. "Mama told me he liked skinny women whose breasts were just a bit too big for their bodies. He had a long nose, too, like yours. Did I ever tell you how he died?"

"No, sugar, you didn't that I recall."

"He got lead-poisoned from cleanin' the old paint off our house without usin' a mask. Mama said his brain just fell apart in pieces. Started he couldn't remember things? Got real violent? Finally in the middle of one night he poured kerosene over himself and lit a match. Near burned down the house with me and Mama asleep upstairs. We got out just in time. It was a year before I met you."

Sailor took the cigarette out of Lula's hand and put it into the ashtray by the bed. He put his hands on her small, nicely muscled shoulders and kneaded them.

"How'd you get such good shoulders?" Sailor asked.

"Swimmin', I guess," said Lula. "Even as a child I loved to swim."

Sailor pulled Lula to him and kissed her throat.

"You got such a pretty, long neck, like a swan," he said.

"Grandmama Pace had a long, smooth white neck," said Lula. "It was like on a statue it was so white? I like the sun too much to be white like that."

Sailor and Lula made love, and afterward, while Sailor slept, Lula stood at the window and smoked one of Sailor's Camels while she stared at the tail of the Cape Fear River. It was a little spooky, she thought, to be at the absolute end of a body of water. Lula looked over at Sailor stretched out on his back on the bed. It was odd that a boy like Sailor didn't have any tattoos, she thought. His type usually had a bunch. Sailor snorted in his sleep and turned onto his side, showing Lula his long, narrow back and flat butt. She took one more puff and threw the cigarette out the window into the river.

UNCLE POOCH

"FIVE YEARS AGO?" Lula said. "When I was fifteen? Mama told me that when I started thinkin' about sex I should talk to her before I did anything about it."

"But honey," said Sailor, "I thought you told me your Uncle Pooch raped you when you were thirteen."

Lula nodded. She was standing in the bathroom of their room at the Cape Fear Hotel fooling with her hair in front of the mirror. Sailor could see her through the doorway from where he lay on the bed.

"That's true," Lula said. "Uncle Pooch wasn't really an uncle. Not a blood uncle, I mean. He was a business partner of my daddy's? And my mama never knew nothin' about me and him for damn sure. His real name was somethin' kind of European, like Pucinski. But everyone just called him Pooch. He came around the house sometimes when Daddy was away. I always figured he was sweet on Mama so when he cornered me one afternoon I was surprised more than a little."

"How'd it happen, peanut?" Sailor asked. "He just pull out the old toad and let it croak?"

Lula brushed away her bangs and frowned. She took a cigarette from the pack on the sink and lit it, then let it dangle from her lips while she teased her hair.

"You're terrible crude sometimes, Sailor, you know?" Lula said.

"I can't hardly understand you when you talk with one of them Mores in your mouth," said Sailor.

Lula took a long slow drag on her More and set it down on the edge of the sink.

"I said you can be too crude sometimes. I don't think I care for it."

"Sorry, sugar," Sailor said. "Go on and tell me how old Pooch done the deed."

"Well, Mama was at the Busy Bee havin' her hair dyed? And I was alone in the house. Uncle Pooch come in the side door through the porch, you know? Where I was makin' a jelly and banana sandwich? I remember I had my hair in curlers 'cause I was goin' that night with Vicky and Cherry Ann, the DeSoto sisters, to see Van Halen at the Charlotte Coliseum. Uncle Pooch must have known nobody but me was home 'cause he come right in and put both his hands on my butt and sorta shoved me up against the counter."

"Didn't he say somethin'?" said Sailor.

Lula shook her head and started brushing the teases out of her hair. She picked up her cigarette, took a puff and threw it into the toilet. The hot end had burned a brown stain on the porcelain of the sink and Lula licked the tip of her right index finger and rubbed it but the stain wouldn't come off.

"Not really," she said. "Least not so I recall now."

Lula flushed the toilet and watched the More come apart as it swirled down the hole.

"What'd he do next?" asked Sailor.

"Stuck his hand down my blouse in front."

"What'd you do?"

"Spilled the jelly on the floor. I remember thinkin' then that Mama'd be upset if she saw it. I bent down to wipe it up and that got Uncle Pooch's hand out of my shirt. He let me clean up the jelly and throw the dirty napkin I used in the trash before doin' anything else."

"Were you scared?" Sailor asked.

"I don't know," said Lula. "I mean, it was Uncle Pooch. I'd known him since I was seven? I kind of didn't believe it was really happenin'."

"So how'd he finally nail you? Right there in the kitchen?"

"No, he picked me up. He was short but powerful. With hairy arms? He had a sort of Errol Flynn mustache, kind of a few narrow hairs on the rim of his upper lip. Anyway, he carried me into the maid's dayroom, which nobody used since Mama lost Abilene a couple years before when she run off to marry Sally Wilby's driver Harlan and went to live down in Tupelo? We did it there on Abilene's old bed."

" 'We' did it?" said Sailor. "What do you mean? Didn't he force you?"

"Well, sure," said Lula. "But he was super gentle, you know? I mean he raped me and all, but I guess there's all different kinds of rapes. I didn't exactly want him to do it but I suppose once it started it didn't seem all that terrible."

"Did it feel good?"

Lula put down her hairbrush and looked in at Sailor. He was lying there naked and he had an erection.

"Does my tellin' you about this get you off?" she said. "Is that why you want to hear it?"

Sailor laughed. "I can't help it happenin', sweetheart. Did he do it more than once?"

"No, it was over pretty quick. I didn't feel much. I'd broke my own cherry by accident when I was twelve? When I came down hard on a water ski at Lake Lanier in Flowery Branch, Georgia. So there wasn't any blood or nothin'. Uncle Pooch just stood and pulled up his trousers and left me there. I stayed in Abilene's bed till I heard him drive off. That was the bad part, lyin' there listenin' to him leave."

"What'd you do then?"

"Went back in the kitchen and finished makin' my sandwich, I guess. I probably took a pee in between or somethin'."

"And you never told nobody about it?"

"Just you," Lula said. "Uncle Pooch never acted strange or different after. And he never did anything else to me. I always got a nice present from him at Christmas, like a coat or jewelry? He died in a car crash three years later while he was holidayin' in Myrtle Beach. They still got way too much traffic there for my taste."

Sailor stretched an arm toward Lula. "Come on over to me," he said.

Lula went and sat on the edge of the bed. Sailor's erection had reduced itself by half and she took it in her left hand.

"You don't have to do nothin' for me, baby," said Sailor. "I'm okay."

Lula smoothed back her hair with her right hand.

"Damn it, Sailor," she said, "it's not always you I'm thinkin' of."

Lula sat still for a minute and then she began to cry. Sailor sat up and held her in his arms and rocked her and didn't say anything until she stopped.

MARIETTA
AND JOHNNIE

"I KNEW THIS WOULD HAPPEN. Soon as that piece of filth got out of Pee Dee I knew there'd be trouble. He's just got some kind of *influence* over her I can't decipher. There's somethin' wild in Lula I don't know *where* it come from. You gotta find 'em, Johnnie, and shoot that boy. Just kill him and dump the body in a swamp. Eliminate the problem once and *for* all."

Johnnie Farragut grinned and shook his head.

"Now, Marietta, you know I can't kill Sailor."

"Why in blazes not? He killed a man, didn't he? That Somethin' Somethin' Lemon person?"

"And he served his time for it. Another thing: If Lula is with him of her own volition—willingly, that is—there ain't much can be done about it."

"Don't talk down to me, Johnnie Farragut. I know what *volition* means, and that's why I want Sailor Ripley off the planet! He's pure slime and it's leakin' all over my baby. You could push him into makin' some kinda move and then shoot him dead. You'd only be defendin' yourself and with his record nobody'd fuss."

Johnnie poured himself another tumblerful of Walker Black Label. He held the bottle out toward Marietta but she shook her head no and put a hand over the top of her glass.

"I'll locate Lula, Marietta, and if she's with the Ripley boy I'll give him a talkin'-to and try to convince her to come back with me. That's about all I can do." He took a long swallow from the tumbler.

Marietta began to cry. She blubbered for a few seconds and then stopped as abruptly as she'd started. Her grey eyes glazed over and turned slightly purple.

"Then I'll hire a hit man," she said. "If you won't help me, I'll call Marcello Santos. He and Clyde were always close."

"Now, Marietta, I *am* goin' to help you. And don't be gettin' carried away. You don't want to be bringin' Santos and his people into it. Besides, he and Clyde weren't gettin' along so well there toward the end."

"It was the lead paint killed Clyde, Johnnie, not Marcello. You know that. And anyway, Marcello Santos has been sweet on me from before I married Clyde. My mama didn't want me to have nothin' to do with him, so I just always kept it polite. Prob'ly I shouldn'ta listened to her. Look at Lula. *She* don't pay me no nevermind."

"Times is different now, Marietta."

"Manners ain't. Might be kids nowadays got it on their mind the world could blow up any second, but seems hardly any of 'em care or know how to act proper anymore."

"I've noticed," said Johnnie. He took a big sip of scotch, leaned all the way back in Clyde Fortune's old Niagara chair, and closed his eyes.

"Lula included," Marietta said. "And mostly it's my own fault. After Clyde died, I tended to indulge Lula more'n I should have, I suppose."

"Yours was not an uncommon reaction, Marietta."

"I understand that, but this obsession she has with this murderer I *don't* understand."

Johnnie belched softly and opened his eyes.

"He ain't a murderer. You got to get off that kick," said Johnnie. "And far's I can tell Sailor was entire clean prior to that event involved Lula. Even there he was protectin' her. Just got too forceful is all."

"Maybe I oughta take a trip, Johnnie. Go to Cairo or Spain or Singapore on one of them tours the Diners Club is always sendin' me brochures about. Think Lula'd go with me?"

"I believe you'd best take things one step at a time, Marietta."

HEAT WAVE

"I USED TO LIKE THE HEAT, Sailor, I really did," said Lula. "But right now I don't care how good it is for my skin. I could use a cool breeze."

Sailor Ripley and Lula Pace Fortune were sitting next to each other in lawn chairs on the porch of the Cape Fear Hotel. It was early evening but the temperature was still in the nineties, down from the high of a hundred and six that had been reached at just past three o'clock in the afternoon.

"Who told you that the heat does anything good for skin?" asked Sailor.

"Magazines, honey. The ones for women? Like you get in the Winn-Dixie by the checkout."

Lula was wearing her yellow one-piece and Sailor was naked except for his blue boxer shorts with white polka dots on them. She stroked his arm nearest her, the left.

"You've got beautiful skin, Sailor. It's so smooth. I just love to trace my fingertips down your arm or back without thinkin', you know? It reminds me of a skier slidin' through perfect white snow."

"It's 'cause I don't go out in no hot sun," said Sailor. "I don't get fried up like you."

"Oh, I know," Lula said. "There's lots of articles now about how many people, kids even, are gettin' skin can-

cer? 'Cause the ozone layer is disappearin'. Seems to me
the government could do somethin' about it."

"How's that?" asked Sailor.

"Keepin' us separated from outer space and all," said
Lula. "One of these mornin's the sun'll come up and burn
a hole clean through the planet like a X ray."

Sailor laughed. "That ain't never will happen, honey,"
he said. "Least not in our lifetime."

"It's the future I'm thinkin' of, Sailor. What if we have
children and they have children? You mean you wouldn't
be upset if some big ol' fireball loosed itself on your
grandkids?"

"Peanut, by that time they'll be drivin' Buicks to the
moon."

Lula stared out at the water. Now that the sun had
completely gone, a beacon from the Cape Fear River
pilot's tower, which was a hundred yards or so south of
the hotel, lit up a path along the channel. Neither Sailor
nor Lula spoke for several minutes. Down the row on
another porch a woman laughed. It was a kind of wild,
crazy laugh, and for the few seconds it lasted Lula
squeezed Sailor's arm as tightly as she could.

"You okay, honey?" Sailor asked, rubbing his arm
where she'd squeezed it.

"I guess so," she said. "I'm sorry I grabbed you so hard
but that woman's laugh creeped me out. It sounded like a
hyena or somethin', didn't it?"

"Never heard one," said Sailor.

"Oh, you know, like on the *National Geographic* TV?"

"Just sounded like an old gal havin' a good time to me."

"Of all the movie stars?" Lula said. "Susan Hayward
had the best laugh. She was all throaty and husky
soundin'. You ever see that old picture on the late movie
she was the woman went to the electric chair or the gas
chamber, I forget which?"

"Nope," said Sailor.

"She was married to this dope addict who beat her up? And she was friends with these robbers and there's a killin' and she's mostly innocent but she ends up with the death sentence anyway. Well, she got to laugh a lot in that one."

"Until they croaked her," Sailor said.

Lula nodded. "Uh huh. But Miss Susan Hayward didn't get cheated on her laugh."

"You hungry yet?" Sailor asked.

"I could eat, probably," said Lula. "But I need me a kiss first, honey. Just one?"

SOUTHERN STYLE

LULA PUT ON HER FAVORITE pink shortie night-gown and snuggled up next to Sailor, who was lying on his stomach with only his undershorts on watching *The Dating Game* on the television.

"What you want to watch this silliness for?" Lula asked. "Ain't one of those people have a real thought in their brain."

"That so?" said Sailor. He kept his gaze on the TV. "You want to tell me what if any real thoughts you had lately?"

"What you have to get personal about so quick?" said Lula. "All I mean is you could possibly read a book or somethin'. I hate the way people look and act on TV? They're like puffed-up dolls? And sick lookin', especially in color. People are better off in black-and-white."

Sailor grunted.

"What's that, honey?" said Lula.

"We didn't have no TV up at Pee Dee, baby, you know? They don't make no special A-number-one effort to keep county farm inmates entertained. You kind of have to make do with what you got."

Lula slid her head up and kissed Sailor on the cheek. "I'm sorry, sweetie," she said. "I forget some moments where-all you been the last two years."

"Twenty-three months, eighteen days is all," Sailor said. "Don't need to make more of it than it was."

"While you were away?" said Lula. "Mama insisted on throwin' this dinner party for the Armisteads, some acquaintances of hers from Mississippi. They'd drove up to deliver their daughter, Drusilla, to the college? Sue and Bobby Breckenridge was there also, and Bobby's mother, Alma. Alma must be eighty-six or eighty-seven years old now? She just sat in a corner chair and didn't move or say a syllable. She must be deaf because she never reacted to anythin' anybody said all evenin'. You listenin', Sailor?"

"I been trained to do more'n one thing at a time, peanut, you know that."

"Just checkin', so I know I ain't talkin' for no good reason. Well, Eddie Armistead is just one very tall anteater of a man? Runs a drugstore in Oxford, where he was born and raised. And Mama has all these books by William Faulkner, you know, the writer? Paul Newman was in a old movie of one of 'em? And Lee Remick when she was so young and beautiful? Now she's old and beautiful, of course. So Mama went to visit William Faulkner's house once in Oxford, 'cause it's a museum now I guess, and wound up meetin' the Armisteads."

"What about the wife?" asked Sailor.

"Mrs. Armistead?" said Lula. "Oh, well, she didn't say very much. Elvie, I think that's her name? The anteater did all the talkin'. He said stuff like when he was a boy Mister Bill—that's what he called William Faulkner?—would scold him for runnin' through the tulip beds of his plantation. Rowan Oak, I think it's named. 'You must run around the flowers, Eddie,' the anteater said William Faulkner told him. 'Yes, sir, Mister Bill,' the anteater said he'd say, before runnin' off over William Faulkner's tulip beds again. For some reason my mama thought this was someway humorous.

"Anyway, Sailor, what I wanted to tell you was about the dinner. That was the best part. Drusilla? The daughter? Why, she looked like somethin' you drink through a straw. And when Mama was fillin' her plate for her Drusilla shouted out—so far, like old Alma Breckenridge, she hadn't said a thing all evenin' either—not to let the potatoes touch the meat? Bobby and I just looked at each other and laughed. 'What'd you say?' he asked Drusilla. 'I just couldn't eat at all if they were touchin',' she said. Don't you think that's about the strangest thing you ever heard?"

"Heard stranger," said Sailor. "But she's a case."

Lula clucked her tongue. "And then, later on? After the Armisteads had left? Bobby said Drusilla was the first real Mississippi belle he'd ever met."

On *The Dating Game* a cute blond girl in a short white dress was standing and giggling and hugging a tall cute guy who had lots of dark hair.

"So what's happenin'?" Lula asked.

"This couple's goin' on a date to Hawaii," said Sailor. "The girl chose him over two other guys."

"Don't the reject guys get anythin'?"

"Gift certificates to Kentucky Fried Chicken," Sailor said.

"That don't seem fair," said Lula.

"Hell, why should *The Datin' Game* be different from real life?" asked Sailor. "At least them boys is gonna get somethin' to eat."

THE DIFFERENCE

"I'M NOT SURE what to do about Mama."

Lula was sitting on the edge of the bathtub smoking a More while Sailor stood in front of the sink, shaving.

"What can you do?" said Sailor. "She's been your mama for twenty years and change now. You know she ain't about to change her ways at this late date."

Lula was looking up at the back of Sailor's head, admiring his curly chestnut hair.

"Honey?" she said. "I sure am glad that prison haircut is on its way to growin' out. Gives me somethin' to grab hold of while we're makin' love."

Sailor laughed. "When I was twelve there was a girl lived next door named Bunny Sweet who was a couple or three years older than me. Bunny loved an old hit record, 'Party Doll' by Buddy Knox, and she used to go around singin' it all the time, especially the part where he says, 'run my fingers through your har.' That's how he says it, 'har' not 'hair.' One day Bunny and two friends of hers came up to me and asked if they could run their fingers through my har, like in the song. They liked that it was so long and wavy. These girls were kind of the bad girls in the neighborhood. Hung out with the local hard asses, guys older than them. They were real sexy, you know? So, sure, I told 'em, go ahead. They formed a circle around me and Bunny slid her long, purple nails into my hair, and then her friends did it, too."

"What'd they say when they did it?"

"Somethin' like, 'Ooh, baby, it's so soft!' I remember the tobacco stains on their fingers, the way they smelled from Florida Water and cigarettes. I thought about their hands, that they'd jacked guys off and stuck 'em in their own pussies. I had a hard time standin' still. When they finished they sniffed their fingers, rubbed 'em together and wiped 'em off on their skirts. It got me real excited."

"You never done nothin' more with 'em?" asked Lula. She flicked the ash off her cigarette into the tub.

"Not with those girls, I didn't," said Sailor. "It wasn't much after that time, though, that I went with a buddy to a party at some girl's house I didn't know. We got into a game of spin the bottle and I wound up goin' into a back room with a very proper-lookin', pretty little blond girl wearin' a blue-checked dress. We were supposed to just kiss once and come back out, but it didn't happen that way at all. She had shiny red bee lips and we really got into it, takin' our time and usin' our tongues."

Lula laughed. "That's hell o' raw for twelve years old," she said.

"It was a surprise, too," said Sailor. "For me, anyway. 'Specially from this straight-lookin' chick I ain't never seen before. So after about three or four minutes we hear the kids in the other room hootin' and hollerin' and whistlin'. Both this girl and I were hot, right? And like I say, real surprised by it. 'I guess we better go out now,' she says to me. We were in a kind of storage room, with pieces of furniture all stacked around us, in some dim red light, and her eyes and lips looked huge. She put her hand on the side of my head and real slowly brushed her fingers through my hair. I tried to kiss her again but she dodged it and ran out. I heard the kids hoot and shout even louder when she came back in the other room. I remember startin' to wipe her lipstick off with the back of my hand, but I stopped and decided to leave it there. Then I followed her out."

Lula tossed her More into the toilet. "You know, there's somethin' I ain't never told you about, Sailor. When I was almost sixteen I got pregnant."

Sailor rinsed his face and toweled himself off. He turned around and leaned back against the washbasin.

"You tell your mama?" he asked.

Lula nodded. "She got me an abortion in Miami from some old Jewish doctor with the hairiest nostrils and ears I ever seen. He told me after I'd be able to have kids no problem. He did it in a hotel room on the beach and when we were goin' down in the elevator? And I was almost passin' out and cryin' with my mouth closed? Mama says, 'I hope you appreciate my spendin' six hundred dollars, not countin' what it cost us to get here and back, on Dr. Goldman. He's the finest abortionist in the South.' "

"You tell the boy who knocked you up?"

"It was my cousin, Dell, done it. His folks used to visit with us summers."

"What happened to him?"

"Oh, nothin'. I never let on to Mama about Dell bein' the one. I just flat refused to tell her who the daddy was? I didn't tell Dell, neither. He was back home in Chattanooga by then anyhow, and I didn't see the point. Somethin' terrible happened to him, though. Six months ago."

"What's that, peanut?"

"Dell disappeared. He'd started behavin' weird? Like comin' up to people every fifteen minutes and askin' how they were doin'? And just seemin' real spacey and actin' funny."

"Actin' funny how?" said Sailor.

"Well, like Mama told me Aunt Rootie—Dell's mama?—she found Dell up in the black of night all dressed and makin' sandwiches in the kitchen. Aunt Rootie asked him what he was doin' and Dell told her he was makin' his lunch and goin' to work. He's a welder? And she made him go back to bed. Then he'd carry on about the weather? Talk about how rainfall's controlled by aliens livin' on earth sent as spies from another planet. Also how men wearin' black leather gloves 'cause they got metal hands are followin' him around."

"Prob'ly the rain boys from outer space," Sailor said.

"It ain't so funny now, though," said Lula. "December, before Christmas? Dell disappeared and Aunt Rootie hired a private eye to find him. He was missin' for almost a month before he wandered back in the house one mornin'. Said he'd been drivin' to work and the next thing he knew he was in Sarasota, Florida, on a beautiful beach, so he decided to stay for a while. The private eye cost Aunt Rootie over a thousand dollars? Then a little while later Dell run off again to someplace and nobody seen him since."

"He don't sound so crazy to me," said Sailor. "Probably just he needed to make a change is all."

"One thing about Dell?" Lula said.

"What's that?"

"When he was about seventeen he started losin' his hair."

"So?"

"He's twenty-four now. A year older than you? And he's about bald."

"There's worse things can happen to a man, honey," said Sailor.

"Yeah, I suppose," said Lula. "Hair does make a difference, though."

DIXIE PEACH

SAILOR AND LULA sat at a corner table next to the window in the Forget-Me-Not Cafe sipping their drinks. Lula had an iced tea with three sugars and Sailor had a High Life, which he drank straight from the bottle. They'd both ordered fried oysters and cole slaw and were enjoying the view. There was a nail paring of a moon and the sky was dark grey with streaks of red and yellow and beneath it the black ocean lay flat on its back.

"That water reminds me of Buddy Favre's bathtub," said Sailor.

"How's that?" Lula asked.

"My daddy's duck-huntin' partner, Buddy Favre, used to take a bath ever' evenin'. Buddy was a stumpy guy with a mustache and goatee and kinda slanty eyes so he looked like a devil but he was a regular guy. He was a truck mechanic, worked on big rigs, eighteen-wheelers, and he got awful filthy doin' it. So nights when he got home he soaked himself in a tub full of Twenty Mule Team Borax and the water turned a kind of thick grey and black, like the way the ocean looks tonight. My daddy would go over to Buddy's and sit in a chair in the bathroom and sip I.W. Harper while Buddy bathed, and sometimes he took me with him. Buddy smoked a joint ever' night while he was in the tub. He'd offer it to Daddy but he stuck to the whisky. Buddy said the reefer come from Panama and that he was gonna end up there one day."

"Did he?"

"I don't know, honey. I lost track of him after Daddy died, but Buddy was a pretty determined type of man, so I imagine he'll make it eventually if he ain't already."

"Where'd you get high first, Sailor? You remember?"

Sailor took a long swig of his High Life. "Sure do. I was fifteen and Bobby Tebbetts and Gene Toy—my half-Chinaman friend I told you about?—we was drivin' Bobby's '55 Packard Caribbean to Ciudad Juarez so we could get laid. Bobby'd been down there before when he'd been visitin' some family in El Paso, and he and a cousin of his went over to Juarez and got their peckers wet for the first time. Gene Toy and I got Bobby to talkin' about it one night and we just decided on the spot to get up and go get it done."

"That's an awful long way to go," said Lula, "just to get some pussy."

"We was only—let's see, I was fifteen and Tebbetts was seventeen and a half and Gene Toy was sixteen. I had my first taste on that trip. At that age you still got a lot of energy."

"You still got plenty energy for me, baby. When's the first time you done it with a girl who wasn't hookin'?"

"Maybe two, three months after Juarez," said Sailor. "I was visitin' my cousin, Junior Train, in Savannah, and we were at some kid's house whose parents were out of town. I remember there were kids swimmin' in a indoor pool and some of 'em was standin' around in the yard or the kitchen drinkin' beer. A girl come up to me that was real tall, taller than me, and she had a real creamy complexion but there was a interestin' star-shaped scar on her nose."

"Was it big?"

"No. About thumbnail size, like a tattoo almost."

"So she come up to you?"

"Yeah." Sailor laughed. "She asked me who I was with and I said nobody, just Junior. She asked me did I want a beer and I held up the one I was holdin'. She asked me did I live in Savannah and I said no, I was visitin' family."

"She know them?"

"No. She looked right at me and run her tongue over her lips and put her hand on my arm. Her name was Irma."

"What'd you say to her then?"

"Told her my name. Then she said somethin' like, 'It's so noisy down here. Why don't we go upstairs so we can hear ourselves?' She turned around and led the way. When she got almost to the top step I stuck my hand between her legs from behind."

"Oh, baby," said Lula. "What a bad boy you are!"

Sailor laughed. "That's just what she said. I went to kiss her but she broke off laughin' and ran down the hallway. I found her lyin' on a bed in a room. She was a wild chick. She was wearin' bright orange pants with kind of Spanish-lookin' lacy black stripes down the sides. You know, them kind that doesn't go all the way down your leg?"

"You mean like Capri pants?" said Lula.

"I guess. She just rolled over onto her stomach and stuck her ass up in the air. I slid my hand between her legs again and she closed her thighs on it."

"You're excitin' me, honey. What'd she do?"

"Her face was half pushed into the pillow, and she looked back over her shoulder at me and said, 'I won't suck you. Don't ask me to suck you.' "

"Poor baby," said Lula. "She don't know what she missed. What color hair she have?"

"Sorta brown, blond, I guess. But dig this, sweetie.

Then she turns over, peels off them orange pants, and spreads her legs real wide and says to me, 'Take a bite of peach.' "

Lula howled. "Jesus, honey! You more than sorta got what you come for."

The waitress brought their oysters and slaw.

"Y'all want somethin' more to drink?" she asked.

Sailor swallowed the last of his High Life and handed the bottle to the waitress.

"Why not?" he said.

THE REST OF
THE WORLD

"I'LL DROP MAMA A POSTCARD from some-where," said Lula. "I mean, I don't want her to worry no more than necessary."

"What do you mean by necessary?" said Sailor. "She's prob'ly already called the cops, my parole officer, her p.i. boyfriend—What's his name? Jimmy Fatgut or some-thin'?"

"Farragut. Johnnie Farragut. I suppose so. She knew I was bound to see you soon as you was sprung, but I don't figure she counted on us takin' off together like this."

Sailor was at the wheel of Lula's white '75 Bonneville convertible. He kept it steady at sixty with the top up to avoid attracting attention. They were twenty miles north of Hattiesburg, headed for Biloxi, where they planned to spend the night.

"I guess this means you're breakin' parole, then?" said Lula.

"You guess," Sailor said. "My parole was broke two hundred miles back when we burnt Portagee County."

"What'll it be like in California, Sailor, do you think? I hear it don't rain much there."

"Considerin' we make it, you mean."

"We got through two and a half states already without no problem."

Sailor laughed. "Reminds me of a story I heard at Pee Dee about a guy had been workin' derrick on the Atchafalaya. He hooked up with a prostitute in New Iberia and they robbed a armored car together, killed the driver and the guard, got away with it. The woman done the shootin', too. She planned the whole thing, she told this guy, only she was followin' a plan laid out by her boyfriend who was doin' a stretch for armed robbery up at Angola.

"They were headed for Colorado and had gone north through Arkansas and then over through Oklahoma and were around Enid when who bushwhacks 'em but the boyfriend from Angola. He'd gone over the wall, went lookin' for his old squeeze, and learned about the armored-car robbery. It'd made all the papers because it was so darin' and ingenious. It couldn't have been nobody but her, he figured, 'cause of the way it'd been pulled off, and he'd told her the best route to take to Colorado where the cash could be hid out in a old mine he knew about. He never counted on her attemptin' to pull this gig on her own, of course. It was the score he'd reckoned on makin', maybe usin' her, when he got out of Angola. Anyway, he caught up with 'em before the feds did, and blew 'em both away."

"Nice story, honey," said Lula. "What on earth made you think of it?"

"They'd made it through two and a half states, too, before the road ended."

"What happened to the hardcase from Angola?"

"He got caught by the FBI in Denver and sent back to Louisiana to finish his time on the robbery beef. He's supposed to've stashed the armored-car loot in the Colorado mine. The bodies ain't never turned up."

"Maybe they're buried in the mine, too," said Lula.

"Could be. I heard this from a guy'd done time in Angola. You hear lots of stories in the slam, babe, ain't many of which float. But I buy this one."

Lula lit up a cigarette.

"That don't smell like a More," said Sailor.

"It ain't," said Lula. "I picked me up a pack of Vantages before we left the Cape?"

"They sure do stink."

"Yeah, I guess, but they ain't supposed to be so bad for you."

"You ain't gonna begin worryin' about what's bad for you at this hour, are you, sugar? I mean, here you are crossin' state lines with a A-number-one certified murderer."

"Manslaughterer, honey, not murderer. Don't exaggerate."

"Okay, manslaughterer who's broke his parole and got in mind nothin' but immoral purposes far's you're concerned."

"Thank the Lord. Well, you ain't let me down yet, Sailor. That's more'n I can say for the rest of the world?"

Sailor laughed and shot the Pontiac up to seventy.

"You please me, too, peanut," he said.

ON THE
GULF COAST

"LIFE IS A BITCH and then you marry one."

"What kinda trash talk is that?" said Lula.

Sailor laughed. "What it says on the bumper sticker up front. On that pickup."

"That's disgustin'. Those kinda sentiments shouldn't be allowed out in public. Is this Biloxi yet?"

"Almost. I figure we should find us a place to stay and then go eat."

"Got anyplace special in mind?"

"We oughta stay somewhere outa the way. Not in no Holidays or Ramadas or Motel Six. If Johnnie Farragut's on our trail he'll check those first."

They passed the Biloxi City Limits sign.

"How about that one?" said Lula. "The Host of the Old South Hotel."

"Looks more like the Ghost of the Old South," said Sailor. "We'll try her."

The lobby smelled of fried-chicken grease and there were three old men sitting on straight-backed chairs under the giant ceiling fan watching *The Oprah Winfrey Show* on a big black-and-white television. All three of them looked up at Sailor and Lula when they walked in. There was a giant leafy potted plant that looked like marijuana next to the TV.

"When I was a kid," Sailor whispered to Lula, "my grandaddy showed me a photo of his daddy at a reunion of veterans of the Confederate army. These old geezers over here remind me of that picture. If one or two of 'em had long white beards, they'd look just like them old soldiers in Grandaddy's album. According to Grandaddy, by the time that picture was taken just about all the survivors had promoted theirselfs to general."

The room was small but cheap, sixteen dollars. The plaster on the walls and ceiling was cracked and there was an ancient Motorola TV with rabbit ears hulking in a corner. There was a card table with four plastic glasses and a pink ceramic pitcher on it. In another corner was a decrepit brown bureau and in the middle of the room was an enormous bed with a chipped black headboard. Lula stripped off the dishwater grey bedspread, tossed it over by the bureau and stretched out on the bed.

"I hate hotel bedspreads," she said. "They don't hardly never get washed, and I don't like the idea of lyin' on other people's dirt."

"Come look at this," said Sailor.

Lula got up from the bed and looked out the window. She noticed that the lower left pane was cracked in two places.

"What, honey?" she said.

"There ain't no water in the swimmin' pool. Just a dead tree fell in, prob'ly from bein' struck by lightnin'."

"It's huge. This musta been a grand old place at one time."

Cars zoomed by on the beachfront highway that ran in front of the hotel.

"Lots of servicemen here," said Lula.

"Let's get fed, sweetheart. The light's fadin' fast."

After dinner, Sailor and Lula went for a walk on the

beach. The full moon bleached the sand stark white and turned the Gulf a wrinkled magenta. Lula took off her shoes.

"You really figure Mama got Johnnie Farragut after us?" she said.

"If anyone, it'd be him, honey."

A headless wave rolled up to Lula and she allowed it to wash over her feet. They walked along without talking for a few minutes. The only sounds other than the waves breaking on the beach were cars and trucks honking and racing up on the road.

"You think he'll run us down?" asked Lula.

"Who? Johnnie?"

"Yeah."

"Might. Then again, he'd maybe have better luck findin' Elvis."

"You don't believe Elvis is still alive, do you?" said Lula.

Sailor laughed. "No more'n James Dean is a wrinkled, twisted-up vegetable shut away in a Indiana rest home."

"But you gotta consider all them strange facts. Like the corpse was shorter and weighed less than Elvis?"

"That's just stuff to sell more magazines, sweetheart."

"Well, I wouldn't blame Elvis, though. If he was alive and just wanted to lie low?"

"He's lyin' low okay," said Sailor. "About six feet lower'n we do. Don't concern yourself with it."

Lula clucked her tongue twice. "I heard somethin' awful on the radio the other day," she said. "About this old rock 'n' roll guitarist, he was forty-seven? He got arrested for bein' drunk in Virginia and hanged himself in his cell. Left a wife and seven children. Radio said his daddy was a Pentacostal preacher."

"Guy up at Pee Dee, when he found out a old cell

buddy of his got blown away by the son of a bitch his wife took up with while he was servin' time, said, 'Another derailment on life's railway to heaven.' I don't know, peanut, if maybe we won't get a little lucky."

ORDINARY
COMPANIONS

JOHNNIE'S FIRST MEAL, whenever he was in New
Orleans, was always at The Acme. He got right in the
lunch line and ordered rice and beans with sausages and
an oyster sandwich. After he paid for the food, he set his
tray down on a table by the window and went over to the
bar, where he asked for a Dixie, got it, refused a glass,
paid for the beer and walked back with it to his table.

Johnnie ate half of the oyster sandwich before he took a
man-sized pull off the Dixie. Still the sweetest beer in the
South, he thought, as he swallowed. The polluted river
water gave it that special taste, and no doubt if a body
drank enough of it he would begin to glow in the dark.
That stretch of the Mississippi from Baton Rouge to New
Orleans isn't called the Cancer Corridor for no good
reason. But it sure tasted good on a ninety-eight-degree
day in the Big Easy.

As he ate, Johnnie thought about where, other than
New Orleans, Lula and Sailor might have gone. N.O.
seemed the most likely place, since they could find work
for which they could get paid under the table and fit in
more easily than in Atlanta or Houston. Besides, Lula always liked New Orleans. She'd stayed there many times
with Marietta, mostly at the Royal Sonesta, whenever
Marietta needed to get away on an antiques-shopping

trip. Of course, they could be most anywhere by now: New York, Miami, even on their way to California. But N.O. was a good enough guess for now.

"Do you mind if I share this table?"

Johnnie looked up and saw a large, chocolate-colored man in his late forties or early fifties, wearing a powder blue porkpie hat and holding a tray filled with plates of food, smiling at him.

"The others," said the man, "they are *ocupado*."

"By all means," said Johnnie. "Make yourself to home."

"*Muchas gracias,*" the man said, sitting down. He extended his well-developed right forearm and offered Johnnie a big hand to shake. "My name is Reginald San Pedro Sula. But please do call me Reggie."

Johnnie wiped off his right hand on his napkin and shook.

"Johnnie Farragut," he said. "Pleased to meet ya."

Reggie did not remove his porkpie hat and began eating ferociously, finishing half of his meal before saying anything more.

"You are from New Orleans, Señor Farragut?"

"Johnnie, please. Nope. Charlotte, North Carolina. Here on business."

Reggie smiled broadly, revealing numerous tall, gold teeth. "I am from Honduras. Originally from the Cayman Islands, but now for many years in Honduras. Do you know Honduras, Johnnie?"

"Only that it's supposed to be a pretty poor sight since the hurricane come through last year."

"Yes, that's so. But there is not much to destroy. No big buildings like in New Orleans. Not where I live in the Bay Islands."

"Where is that?"

"North of the mainland. On the island of Utila. We have a certain sovereignty in the islands, you know, since the United States forced the British to give them up over a century ago."

"What do you do there?"

"Oh, many things." Reggie laughed. "I have an appliance shop. But I am also with the government."

Johnnie took a bite of the oyster sandwich.

"In what capacity?" he asked.

"In many capacities. Mostly with the secret service."

Reggie reached into his back pocket and took out his wallet. He handed a card to Johnnie.

" 'General Osvaldo Tamarindo y Ramirez,' " Johnnie read aloud. " 'Teléfono 666.' "

"He is my sponsor," said Reggie. "The general is the head of the secret police of Honduras. I am one of his operatives."

Johnnie handed the card back to Reggie and Reggie gave him a small piece of paper, folded once. Johnnie unfolded it. The printing was in Spanish.

"That is my *permiso*," Reggie said. "My permit to kill. Only if necessary, of course, and only in my own country." He laughed.

"Of course," said Johnnie, refolding the piece of paper and handing it over to Reggie.

"I am authorized to carry a forty-five, also," said Reggie. "United States Marine issue, before they made the unfortunate switch to the less dependable nine millimeters. I have it here, in my briefcase."

Reggie held up his stainless-steel briefcase and then replaced it on the floor beneath his chair.

"Why are you in New Orleans?" asked Johnnie. "If you don't mind my askin'."

Reggie laughed. He took off his hat and scratched

furiously at his completely bald head for a few seconds, wiped the sweat off his scalp with his napkin and put his hat back on.

"Certainly not," Reggie said. "I am here only briefly, in fact, until this evening, when I fly to Austin, Texas, to visit a friend of mine who is an agent for the CIA. He wants to take me bass fishing. He comes to Utila and goes fishing with me. We are in the same businesses and also we are fishermen."

Johnnie swallowed the last of his beer. He'd eaten all he could and stood up to leave. This fellow Reginald San Pedro Sula, Johnnie thought, was undoubtedly telling the truth, but Johnnie had no desire to get into it any deeper.

"It's been a real pleasure, Reggie," he said, extending his hand. "I wish you *buena suerte* wherever you go."

Reggie stood up. He was at least six feet six. He shook Johnnie's hand.

"The same to you," he said. "If you are in Honduras, come to the Bay Islands and visit me. The Hondurans are great friends of the American people. But I have a joke for you before you go. If a liberal, a socialist and a communist all jumped off the roof of the Empire State Building at the same time, which one of them would hit the ground first?"

"I couldn't say," said Johnnie. "Which one?"

"Who cares?" said Reggie, grinning.

Johnnie walked down Iberville Street toward the river. He was eager to get back to his hotel room and read more of Robert Burton's *The Anatomy of Melancholy*. Burton's book, the first treatise on the subject written by a layman, had been published originally in 1621 and was still relevant today. As Johnnie turned the corner and headed north on Decatur, he repeated to himself Burton's definition of melancholy: "A kind of dotage without a fever, having for his ordinary companions fear and sadness, without any apparent occasion."

He'd read for a little while, Johnnie thought, then take a nap. It was more likely he'd run onto Sailor and Lula, if they were here, at night, anyway.

HUNGER
IN AMERICA

"HEAR NOW HOW LEECHES is comin' back into style," said Sailor.

"Say what?" said Lula. "Honestly, sugar, you can talk more shit sometimes?" She took out a cigarette the length and width of a Dixon Ticonderoga No. 2 pencil and lit it.

"Got you a pack of Mores again, huh?"

"Yeah, it's a real problem for me, Sailor, you know. When I went in that drugstore by the restaurant in Biloxi? For the Kotex? I saw 'em by the register and had the girl throw 'em in. I'm not big on resistin'. So what about a leech?"

"Heard on the radio how doctors is usin' leeches again, like in old times. You know, when even barbers used 'em?"

Lula shuddered. "Got one on me at Lake Lanier. Life-guard poured salt on it and it dropped off. Felt awful. He was a cute boy, though, so it was almost worth it."

Sailor laughed. "Radio said back in the 1920s a I-talian doctor figured out that if, say, a fella got his nose mostly bit off in a barfight or somethin', and he needed a skin transplant there, they'd sew one of his forearms to his nose for a few weeks, and when they took it off they'd slap a couple leeches where the new skin attached from his arm to keep the blood movin' so the skin'd stick."

Lula rolled down her window on the passenger side of the front seat of the Bonneville. They were on the outskirts of New Orleans.

"Sailor? You expect me to believe a man'd be goin' around with a arm sewed to his nose? For *weeks*?!"

Sailor nodded. "How they used to do it," he said. "Course they got more sophisticated ways now. Radio said the Chinese, I think it is, figured a better idea is by insertin' a balloon in the forehead and lettin' it hang down on the nose."

Lula shrieked. "Sailor Ripley! You stop! You're makin' this shit up and I ain't gonna sit for it!"

"Honest, Lula," Sailor said. "I prob'ly ain't precisely got all the facts straight, but it's about what they said."

"Honey, here we are in N.O.," said Lula, "and it's time to change the subject."

Sailor pulled off the road into a Gulf gas station minimart.

"We're about dry bones, sweetheart," he said, stopping the car next to a self-serve pump. A sign on the top of it said PLEASE PAY INSIDE BEFORE FUELING.

"Get me a Mounds?" Lula shouted to Sailor as he went into the store.

A tall black man about thirty-five years old, wearing a torn green Tulane tee shirt, grease-stained brown slacks, no socks, ripped tennis shoes and a dirty orange Saints baseball cap, was piling items on the counter by the cash register. In the pile were four ready-made, plastic-wrapped sandwiches, two tuna salad and two cotto salami; six Twinkies; a package of Chips Ahoy chocolate chip cookies; four Slice sodas; two Barq's root beers; and a large package of fried pork rinds, extra salted.

"Sorry, gentlemen," the man said to Sailor and another guy who'd come in right behind Sailor and was also waiting to pay for gas, "I'm 'most finished on my shoppin' here."

"This be it?" the old guy behind the counter said.

"Y'all take American Express?" asked the man.

"Yessir," said the old guy. He had on a green Red Man chewing tobacco cap and a faded blue, short-sleeved attendant's work shirt with the name Erv sewn in black cursive above the chest pocket.

"Then lemme throw in a couple more things," said the man.

Sailor and the man in line behind him watched as the black man gathered up several more packages of Twinkies along with a few cupcakes and half a dozen cans of Pretty Kitty cat food, three liver and three chicken dinner portions, and tossed them on his pile.

"Pussycats gotta eat, too," he said to Sailor, smiling. He had no upper teeth that were visible.

He handed an American Express card to the clerk, who ran it through the verifier. The card checked out okay and the old guy prepared a charge slip, had the man sign it and bagged the purchases.

"I'd just soon have a paper bag rather than a plastic one, if it's same to you," the man said to the clerk.

"We don't have no paper bags," the old guy said, shoving the plastic bag he'd filled toward the man.

"Thanks for waitin', gentlemen," the man said to Sailor and the other patron, picked up his bag and walked out.

"All I want's ten bucks regular," Sailor said to the old guy. "Oh yeah, and a Mounds bar." He took one off the candy and gum rack next to the register and handed the clerk a twenty-dollar bill.

"I ain't got my American Express card with me," he said, "so I got to use cash. Hope that's okay."

Sailor smiled at the old guy but the clerk kept a poker face and just gave him his change. The guy in line behind Sailor shook his head and grinned.

"That took long enough," Lula said when Sailor got back to the car. "You forget my Mounds?"

Sailor tossed her the candy bar.

"I think the country done changed just a little while I was away, peanut," he said.

Lula sank her small white teeth into the chocolate-covered coconut.

"You got to keep an eye on it," she said as she chewed. "That's sure."

By the time Sailor finished pumping the gas, Lula had polished off both sections of the Mounds bar.

"Hope you don't mind I didn't save none for you," Lula said as Sailor climbed back into the driver's seat. "I was dyin'?"

BIRDS DO IT

"I LOVE IT WHEN YOUR EYES GET WILD, honey. They light up all blue almost and spin like pinwheels and little white parachutes pop out of 'em."

Sailor and Lula had just finished making love in their room at the Hotel Brazil on Frenchmen Street.

"Oh, Sailor, you're so *aware* of what goes on with me? I mean, you pay at*tention*. And I swear, you got the sweetest cock. Sometimes it's like it's talkin' to me when you're inside? Like it's got a voice all its own. You get right *on* me."

Lula lit a cigarette and got up from the bed and walked over to the window. She stuck her head outside and craned her neck around but she couldn't quite see the river. Lula sat naked on the end of the table under the open window, staring out and smoking.

"Enjoyin' the view?" Sailor said.

"I was just thinkin' about how people oughta fuck more in the daytime. I don't think there'd be so much trouble about it if they did."

"What kinda trouble?"

"Oh, I don't know. Just seems like people make more of a big deal out of it at night? Get all sorts of exotic expectations, I guess, and things go strange in 'em. It checks out simpler in daylight's what I think."

"You're prob'ly right, sweetie," said Sailor. He yawned,

then threw off the sheet that had been covering him and stood up. "Let's go down and get somethin' to eat, okay? Otherwise, I won't make it past dark."

Sailor and Lula sat at the counter in Ronnie's Nothin' Fancy Cafe on Esplanade, drinking double-size cups of Community coffee. Lula picked apart a giant jelly doughnut, licking the powdered sugar off her fingers. A man on the stool next to Sailor lit up a rum-soaked crook.

Sailor said to him, "My grandaddy used to smoke crooks. Wolf Brothers."

"Used to cost seven cents apiece," the man said. "Now they're five for a buck. Buck and a half some places. Want one?"

"No, thanks," said Sailor, "not while I'm eatin'."

"George Kovich," said the man, extending a gnarled, liver-spotted hand, the knuckles of which looked as if they'd been broken more than once. "You mighta heard of me."

Sailor shook his hand. "Sailor Ripley. This woman is Lula Pace Fortune."

Lula nodded and smiled at George Kovich.

"Pleased to meet you, young lady," Kovich said.

"Don't know that I have," said Sailor. "Should I know about you for anything in particular?"

"Was in all the papers a while back. Two—no, three years now. I'm seventy-six, was only seventy-three then. Had a business in Buffalo, New York, called Rats With Wings. Killed pigeons for anyone who wanted 'em killed. Did *hand*somely, *real* handsomely, for three or four months, till I got shut down."

"Why were you killin' pigeons, Mr. Kovich?" asked Lula. "Were you in the exterminatin' business?"

"No, ma'am, I was a housepainter, in the union forty-one years. I'm retired now, livin' with my sister, Ida. Ida moved down here twenty-five years ago, married an oil man named Smoltz, Ed Smoltz. He's dead now, so it's just me and Ida. I sold my house and moved down after the city of Buffalo put me out of business. Hell, RWW was doin' them a service, and they charged me with endangerin' the public."

"Tell us about the pigeons, Mr. Kovich," said Lula.

"They're useless pests. I've shot hundreds of 'em. My neighbors hired me to get rid of the pigeons that gathered on their roofs and porches and made noise and left droppings all over. I was doin' a job, a good one. Shot a hundred ten of them flyin' rodents just on my own in a couple of days. Neighbors asked me how come the spotted bastards didn't light on my house or my brother Earl's anymore, and I told 'em the truth. I shot 'em. Earl's gone now. Heart attack six months ago. His widow, Mildred, she still lives in the house next to mine. She's stone deaf but the racket the pigeons made drove Earl crazy. He could hear 'em even with the TV on. He owned a bar thirty years, the Boilermaker, on Wyoming Street. Earl's roof was a favorite spot for pigeons. They lit there day and night. I wanted to toss a grenade up there."

"If your neighbors didn't mind," said Sailor, "how'd you get put out of business?"

"Woman drivin' down the street spotted me on a roof with my rifle. She called the police and they came out and arrested me. Thought I was a sniper! Seventy-three years old! Boys at the VFW loved that one. Cops didn't understand about the pigeons, the damage they do to personal property. I used to complain to the city but they never lifted a finger. I was gonna put out poison, but I was afraid somebody's cat would eat it. Hell, I had six cats myself. So I used the twenty-two because it didn't make much noise and the ammo was cheap."

"What happened on the charges?" asked Sailor.

"Guilty on a reduced charge. Hundred-dollar fine and ordered to desist. Pigeons carry diseases and muss up the place. You seen it. Plain filth."

Kovich stood up and put some money on the counter. He was a large man, six two even though he was slightly stoop shouldered. For a man in his seventies he exuded a surprisingly powerful presence. He looked strong.

"It's a serious situation," he said. "Not like the Turks and the Armenians, maybe, or the Arabs and the Jews, but I want people to remember me and what I've done and pick up where I left off. Somebody had to make a move. It was nice meetin' you folks. Ida's expectin' me."

After George Kovich had gone, Lula ordered another jelly doughnut and more coffee.

"Once in the Variety Do-Nut?" she said to Sailor. "I saw a big ol' roach crawl across a creme-fill I was gonna take? When I told the girl workin' there about it she said she was sorry, but even though she wanted to, she just couldn't charge me any less for that one. If Mr. Kovich'd been there he prob'ly woulda just taken out his gun and drilled that bug on the spot."

SPEED TO BURN

"'I DON'T LOCOMOTE NO MORE.'"

"What's that?" said Sailor. "You don't what?"

"I'm just readin' here? In the *Times-Picayune*?" said Lula. "About Little Eva, who sung that song 'The Loco-motion' that was a hit before we was even born?"

"Still a good one," Sailor said. "What's it say?"

"'Little Eva's doin' a brand-new dance now,'" Lula read. "'"I don't locomote no more," said Eva Boyd as she wiped the counter at Hanzies Grill, a soul food restaurant in Kingston, N.C. It's been twenty-five years since Boyd, as teen-aged Little Eva, hit the top of the charts with "The Locomotion." "I ain't into singin' over chicken," the forty-three-year-old Boyd said in a recent interview. She still sings with a gospel group from her church and is considerin' makin' a record. "She sounds beautiful," said waitress Loraine Jackson.'"

"Good to know she ain't quit singin'," said Sailor. "It's a gift."

Sailor and Lula were sitting on a bench by the Missis-sippi watching the barges and freighters glide by. It was late evening but the sky was plum colored, soft and light.

"I don't think we should hang around too long in N.O.," Sailor said. "This is likely the first place they'll come lookin'."

Lula folded the newspaper and put it down next to her on the bench.

"I don't see what Mama can do about us," she said. "Seems to me unless she has me kidnapped, there's no way I'm goin' back without you. And you'd just get popped for violatin' parole if you do. So, there ain't much choice now."

"You know Dimwit Taylor, guy hangs around front of Fatty's Dollar-Saver?"

"Sure. He don't have no teeth and's always smilin' so ugly and sayin', 'Man ain't lonesome long's he got a dog.' Only he ain't got no dog?"

"The one."

"What about him?"

"You ever sit down and talk with him?"

"Not hardly. Always looks like he just crawled out of a pit. Smells it, too."

"He used to be a ballplayer, professional, mostly on barnstormin' teams around the South. Told me once in Alabama, like forty years ago, he was playin' in a game against a black team from Birmin'ham had an amazin' young center fielder could grab anythin' hit his way. There wasn't no outfield fence at the field they was playin' at, so nobody on Dimwit's team could put the ball over this kid's head. He'd just spin, run out from under his cap and take it out of the air like a piece of dust. After the game, Dimwit talks to the boy, turns out he's only fifteen years old."

"What's this got to do with us bein' on the run?"

"That's just it," said Sailor. "Dimwit asked the kid how'd he know just where to head soon's the ball's hit, so he'd snatch it before it touched the ground. And the kid said, 'I got the range and the speed to change.' Dimwit said the kid had it exactly right, and he made it to the big leagues, too."

"So you figure you got the range, huh?"

Sailor laughed. "I do, peanut. I just got to trust myself, is all. And I got speed to burn."

Lula pushed herself right up against Sailor and rested her head on his chest.

"I like how you talk, Sailor. And you know what? I believe you, I really, really do."

LOCUS CERULEUS

ON HIS FIRST NIGHT IN NEW ORLEANS, Johnnie Farragut sat on a stool in Snug Harbor watching the Braves lose again on TV, this time to the St. Louis Cardinals. A guy down the bar was complaining loudly about the ineptitude of the Atlanta team.

"The Cards ain't got a guy on the team can poke a ball past the infield, and the Braves still can't beat 'em," the man shouted. "Murphy must be a saint, stickin' with this outfit. He could be playin' in New York, L.A., anywhere, makin' his two million on a winnin' club."

"Maybe he likes the weather in Atlanta," said someone else.

"Yeah, and Mother Teresa is carryin' her and Bishop Tutu's love child," said the bartender.

Johnnie ordered his second double Black Label on the rocks and took out his pen and spiral notebook. He'd always wanted to be a writer, especially for television shows like *The Twilight Zone, The Outer Limits* or *One Step Beyond,* programs that, unfortunately, were no longer on the air. Whenever he had an idea for a story, he wrote it down. Just now Johnnie felt a ripple in his locus ceruleus, the area of the brain from which dreams emanate. Johnnie had read about this, and he believed that the locus ceruleus was his center of creativity. He never ignored the signal. Johnnie took his drink and notebook and moved to a booth so that he could concentrate. Finding Sailor and Lula would have to wait.

A GOOD CONNECTION

by Johnnie Farragut

Harry Newman sat on a corner stool in Barney's Tavern, watching the ballgame on TV. An error by the Braves shortstop in the bottom of the ninth gave the game to St. Louis and Harry swore under his breath. He'd put a couple of Jacksons on Atlanta this morning on the long end of five to two; a good bet, he'd figured. Lousy luck was all it was, he thought. All the guy had to do was keep his glove down, flip the ball to second for the force, and that was it. Instead, the ball goes through, all the way to the wall, two runners score, and that's the name of that tune.

Harry swallowed the last of his beer and slid off the stool. Barney came over behind the bar. "Tough luck, Harry," he said. "You oughta know better. The Braves never have no good luck in St. Louis." "Yeah, and I never have no good luck anyplace," said Harry, as he headed out the door. "That guy," Barney said to the customer who'd been sitting at the bar next to Harry, "he just don't know how to bet, is all. Loses ten times for every one he wins." "Some guys are like that," said the customer. "They never learn."

Harry walked downtown, shuffling along, not sure of where he was headed. He almost bumped into someone, excused himself, looked up, and that's when he saw it: a bright yellow 1957 Buick convertible. It was cherry, in perfect condition, sitting in the front row of

Al Carson's used-car lot. Harry went right to it and ran his hand over the right front fender, then stroked up and along the top. It was the most gorgeous automobile he'd ever seen.

"She's somethin', ain't she, Harry?" said Al Carson, who'd come up behind him. Harry didn't even turn around to look at the wizened little car dealer. He just couldn't take his eyes off the old Buick. "She sure is," said Harry. "It looks brand-new." "Just about," said Al. "Only a fraction more than 15,000 miles on her in thirty years. A little old lady kept it in her garage. Only drove it to church on Sundays and to see her sister across town twice a month. Hard to believe, I know, but true." "How much, Al?" asked Harry. "How much do you want for her?" "Three grand," said Al. "But for you, Harry, make it twenty-seven fifty." "I've got about forty bucks on me now, Al," said Harry. "How about if you take that and I'll pay you a hundred a month?" "I don't know, Harry," Al said, shaking his tiny bald head. "Your credit ain't been at the top of the list lately." "Oh, come on, Al. I'll pay you. I will. I've just got to have this beauty."

Harry walked around the car, opened the driver's side door and got in. "Hey, what's this?" he said. "A telephone? They didn't have telephones in many cars over thirty years ago!" "Doesn't work, of course," said Al. "Don't know that it ever did. Doesn't appear it was ever really hooked up to nothing. I bought the car from the old woman's son and he couldn't tell me about it, either. Just said he always thought it was odd, too. What'd the old lady need a phone in her car for, anyway?" Al laughed. "I guess I should charge you extra for it!"

Harry slid back out and handed his two twenties to Al. "Come on, Al. You can trust me for it. You know me. I ain't gonna go run nowhere and hide." "You don't ever have enough dough to go nowhere!" said Al.

"But I guess I can let you take it. Come on in the office and sign the paper and you can drive it out right now. She runs real good."

Harry drove his cherry 1957 Buick all over town that day, showing it off to everybody, proud as could be. After cruising around the neighborhood a few times he decided to take it out into the country for a real spin, to cut it loose and see what she could do on the open road. Not far past the city limits it began to rain. Harry put on the windshield wipers and they worked just fine, humming away as they cleared the water from view. Harry gave the Buick the gun, hurtling along the highway like a yellow flame. Rounding a curve, however, the tires hit a slick spot and the Buick spun out of Harry's control. He fought to keep the car on the road but it wobbled, slid and finally flew off the side into a ditch. The impact knocked Harry out.

"This is the operator. How may I help you? Hello, this is the operator speaking. How may I be of assistance?" Harry came to slowly, awakened by the sound of a voice. Someone was speaking to him. But who? He shook his head, opened his eyes, and saw that the telephone receiver had fallen off the hook. "Hello? Hello? This is the operator. What number do you want?" The voice was coming from the car phone. Harry shook his head again. He thought this must be his imagination, that his head was full of cobwebs from the crash. But no, it was the operator talking.

Harry picked up the receiver. "Hello," he said. "Operator? I'm sorry, I . . . I've just been in an accident and I'm stuck in a ditch. I mean my car is stuck. I must have lost control in the storm and gone off the road. Yes, I'm all right, I think," he told her. "Where am I?" Harry struggled around in the seat to look out the window. The rain had stopped. "About fifteen miles past the city limits, I guess. On the old Valley Road. Could you call a

tow truck for me? Yes, certainly, Operator. I'll hold on."
Harry shook his head again and felt his shoulder, his
legs. He seemed to be in one piece, not seriously hurt.
Another voice came on the line. "Bud's Service Station?
Right, yes, well, I've had an accident. She told you?
Twenty minutes? Great, great. No, I guess I'll be here all
right." Harry hung up the telephone and stared at it.

Twenty minutes later a truck pulled up. The lettering
on the sides of the doors of the cab said BUD'S TOW 24
HOURS. A large man, about fifty years old, with a two-
day growth of beard and an unlit cigar stub stuck in his
mouth, climbed down out of the cab and came over to
where Harry was standing beside the Buick. The man
wore a dark blue work shirt with the sleeves rolled
partway up each meaty forearm. The name Bud was
emblazoned above the left front pocket.

"They don't make these new buggies like the old
ones," Bud said, as he looked the Buick over. Harry
laughed. "That's pretty good," said Harry. "She was
holding the road pretty well until that curve back
there." Bud grunted and bent down to look at the right
front wheel that was twisted halfway around. Bud
grunted again as he raised himself back up. "Yeah, I
keep my daddy's old '36 Packard runnin'," he said.
"Now that's an automobile that won't let you down so
long as you take care of it. They just churn these babies
out now in too much of a hurry. They don't make 'em
to last. Well, let's see if we can get her out of this," said
Bud, as he walked back to the tow truck.

Bud had the Buick up and out of the ditch in ten
minutes. "Hop up in the cab," he told Harry. "We'll
take her back to the station and get that wheel straight-
ened out." Harry and Bud climbed into the truck and
Bud started off toward town. He reached over and
snapped on the radio. "Say," he said, "I noticed that
telephone in the car. You rig that up yourself? What is

it, shortwave?" Harry nodded, confused. "No, er . . . yes, yeah, that's it."

The truck radio buzzed as it warmed up and Bud fiddled with the dial as he drove. "Got to hear the game. Who're you bettin' on? The Braves or the Yanks?" "What?" asked Harry. "In the Series, it starts today, you know. I like Milwaukee myself. Spahn and Burdette are gonna be tough to beat in a short Series," said Bud. "But I'm afraid of that crafty little lefty, Ford. I'm pretty sure of one thing, though." "What's that?" asked Harry, still trying to figure out what was going on. "That bum Larsen won't pitch another perfect game like he did last year." Bud laughed. "I'd bet the station on that!"

"But Larsen pitched his perfect game in the '56 Series!" said Harry. "That's right, pal," Bud answered. "Like I said, last year. Probably nobody'll do that again in our lifetime, I'll bet." Just then the radio kicked in, and the voice of Mel Allen, the New York Yankees' announcer, filled the cab of the truck. "Welcome to the broadcast of the World Series," said Mel Allen in his unmistakable, mellifluous drawl. "It's a beautiful afternoon here on October second, nineteen hundred and fifty-seven, as the Milwaukee Braves and the New York Yankees prepare to do battle in the House that Ruth Built."

Harry rubbed his head, unable to speak. Then he relaxed and began to smile, suddenly comfortable with the situation. "So whaddaya think?" asked Bud. "The Braves'll win it in seven games," Harry said. "You can bet on it." "That's what I wanted to hear!" said Bud, pounding a fist on the steering wheel. Harry just grinned and watched the road. As the truck passed the City Limits sign, Harry said, "I might put a few bucks down on the Braves myself. Yeah, I think I'll do just that."

ANIMAL LIFE

"DID YOU KNOW THAT MY MAMA was a runner-up for Miss Georgia Chick in 1963?" asked Lula.

"No, sweetheart, I didn't. But I thought you had to be from Georgia to be in a contest like that," said Sailor.

"She was livin' in Valdosta then, with my Great-Aunt Eudora, Aunt Rootie's mama. You remember Rootie, she's Cousin Dell's mama? Dell went crazy and disappeared a while back? Anyways, this is from the time before she married Daddy, which wasn't until 1968. Every year there's this beauty pageant in Gainesville, Georgia. Used to be, anyhow. And Eudora's dear friend, Addie Mae Audubon? Who was a descendant of the man who invented bird watchin'? She got Mama into it. I got the sterlin' silver bracelet the judges give her in my jewelry box back home. Says on it, 'Miss Georgia Chick Contest, 1963,' engraved."

"What'd the winner get?"

"Prob'ly a car or somethin'. Trip to Miami Beach, maybe? When I asked her about it, Mama said she didn't win 'cause her tits wasn't big enough for the one-piece bathin' suit she wore. But she had the best teeth, she said. The girl that won? Mama told me her teeth were almost as big as her tits. I saw a photo of the contest with Miss Georgia Chick holdin' a box of baby roosters. Mama was standin' right beside her."

"You know what they do with 'em?" asked Sailor.

"With what? The baby roosters?"

"Uh huh. Grind 'em up for fertilizer. Only hens make good fryers."

Lula made a face. "Oh, Sailor, that's so sad. Killin' all them babies like that."

"What they do, though," said Sailor.

"Well, Mama said the place stunk terrible. The whole town of Gainesville. From the chicken business? She never has forgot it. The next year Mama moved back up home."

Sailor and Lula hadn't gone to sleep yet, though it was almost four o'clock in the morning. They were lying in bed in their room at the Hotel Brazil, holding hands. A blue snake of light from the streetlamp curled in under the window shade and stretched across their bodies.

"Sailor?"

"Honey?"

"Ever imagine what it'd be like to get eaten alive by a wild beast?"

"Mean a tiger?"

"Yeah. Sometimes I think it'd be the biggest thrill?"

Sailor laughed. "It better be, darlin', 'cause it'd be the last."

"Ripped apart by a gorilla, maybe," said Lula.

"How about bein' squeezed to death by a python?"

Lula shook her head. "I don't think so. That might be way too slow? And you'd feel your ribs crackin' and insides oozin' out. I'd rather get grabbed sudden and pulled apart quick by a real powerful animal."

"Lula, sometimes I gotta admit you come up with some weird thoughts."

"Anythin' interestin' in the world come out of some-body's weird thoughts, Sailor. Couldn't have been no simple soul dreamed up voodoo, for an instance."

"Voodoo?"

"Sure. How else you explain stickin' pins in dolls to make a person squirm or have a heart attack? Or cookin' someone's fingernail clippin's to make 'em vomit till they ain't got nothin' left inside and drop dead. You tell me, Sailor, who could come up with shit like that ain't super weird?"

"You got me, peanut."

"You certain?"

"I ain't never met anyone come close to you, sugar." Lula rolled over on top of Sailor.

"Take a bite of Lula," she said.

SAILOR'S DREAM

"HE'S HERE," SAID LULA. "Johnnie Farragut? I seen him."

"Where?" asked Sailor.

"Over at the Cafe du Monde. He was sittin' at a table outside, eatin' doughnuts."

"He see you?"

"I don't think so. I was comin' out of the praline shop across the street? And I spotted him and come right back here to the hotel. I guess this means we'd best scoot, huh, Sailor?"

"I s'pose, sugar. Come sit next to me a minute."

Lula set her box of pralines on the dresser and sat down on the bed by Sailor.

"We'll be okay, honey. I'll go down do a oil change and we'll hit it."

"Sailor?"

"Uh huh?"

"Recall the time we was sittin' one night behind the Confederate soldier? Leanin' against it. And you took my hand and put it on your heart and you said, 'You feel it beatin' in there Lula get used to it 'cause it belongs to you now.' D'you recall that?"

"I do."

Lula put her head down in Sailor's lap and he stroked her smooth black hair.

"I was hopin' you would. I know that night by heart.

Sometimes, honey? I think it's the best night of my life. Really."

"We didn't do nothin' special I can remember. Just talked, is all."

"Talkin's good. Long as you got the other? I'm a big believer in talkin', case you ain't noticed."

"I had a dream while you were gone," said Sailor. "It's strange, but when I was up at Pee Dee I didn't hardly dream. Maybe a couple or three times, and then nothin' I could remember. About girls, I guess, like ever'body is in."

"You remember this one?"

"Real clear. It wasn't no fun, Lula. I was in a big city, like New York, though you know I ain't never been there. It was winter, with ice and snow all over. I was stayin' in some little ol' rathole with my mama. She was real sick and I had to score some medicine for her, only I didn't have no money. But I told her anyway I'd go get the pills she needed. So I was out in the streets and there was about ten million people comin' and goin' in all directions, and it was impossible for me to keep walkin' straight, to get to wherever it was I was goin'. The wind was blowin' super hard and I wasn't dressed warm. Only instead of freezin', I was sweatin', sweatin' strong. The water was rollin' off me. And I was dirty, too, like I hadn't had no bath in a long time, so the sweat was black almost."

"Boy, sweetie, this is weird okay."

"I know. I kept walkin', even though I didn't have no money for the medicine or a good idea of where to go. People kept pushin' me and knockin' into me, and they was all dressed up for the cold weather. I guess they figured me for a bum or head case, seein' as how I was so filthy and dressed wrong. Then I thought of you and headed for your house. Only it wasn't your house really, it was in this cold, dark New York City, and it was a long way there.

"I was strugglin' ever' step of the way. Pushin' through the crowds. There was more and more people and the sky seemed like it was daytime, only it was dark, too. You were livin' in some big buildin' and I had to go up lots of stairs, but finally I found where it was. You let me in only you weren't real pleased to see me. You kept sayin', 'Why'd you come to see me now? Why now?' Like it'd been a long time since we seen each other."

"Oh, baby, what an idea. I'd always be happy to see you, no matter what."

"I know, peanut. But it wasn't all like you were so unhappy I was there, just you were upset. My bein' there was upsettin' to you. You had short hair, too, and chopped off in front. You had some kids there, little kids, and I guess you'd got married and your husband was comin' home any minute. I tell you, Lula, I was shakin' wet. All this black sweat was pourin' off me, and I knew I was scarin' you, so I took off. And then I woke up, sweatin', and a couple minutes later you come in."

Lula slid her head up to Sailor's chest and put her arms around him.

"Sometimes dreams just don't mean nothin'? What I think, anyway. Stuff come into your mind you don't got no control over, you know? It just come in there and ain't nobody knows for sure why. Like I dreamed once a man stole me and locked me in a room in a tower with one tiny window and there was nothin' but water outside? When I told Mama about it she said it was somethin' I remembered from a story I heard as a child."

"Well, I ain't upset about it, darlin'," said Sailor. "Just give me a odd feelin' there a minute is all."

Lula lifted her head and kissed Sailor under his left ear.

"Dreams ain't no odder than real life," she said. "Sometimes not by half."

THE POLISH
FATHER

JOHNNIE FARRAGUT sat on a bench in Jackson Square watching a pair of tourists take photos of one another. The couple spoke a language Johnnie did not recognize. Croatian, maybe, he thought, although he didn't know what Croatian sounded like. The man and woman were short and stout, probably in their thirties, though they looked older. Their clothes hung loosely from their bodies, obviously not having been tailored to order. After several turns each of posing and shooting, which entailed a considerable amount of heated discussion and dramatic gesticulation, the couple left the park.

As they waddled away, arguing in their grumbling language, Johnnie was reminded of a man who had lived down the street from him for a while when he was a boy. The man, whose name Johnnie could not remember, was Polish, and he had two sons, both round-faced, straw-haired kids a few years younger than Johnnie. There was no mother with the family, just a nice old grandmother who spoke only Polish. She and Johnnie would always nod and smile to each other whenever they passed on the street. The father was also round and fat, and he was bald and wore small, wire-rimmed glasses. His kids' faces were always dirty and it seemed as if they were always eating something: apples, cake, candy bars.

The Polish father was building a boat in his yard. Every evening Johnnie heard the man pounding nails into the frame. Many of the neighbors complained about the noise, but the construction continued without respite during the year and a half or so that the Polish family lived there. In his room late at night, Johnnie could hear the hammering and sawing. From what he'd seen of it, Johnnie thought it was to be a sailboat. At about this time, Johnnie remembered, he'd begun to read books at the library such as *Kon-Tiki* and *Clipper Ship Days*. It wasn't until much later that he discovered the novels of Joseph Conrad, who was Polish, and whose real name was Jozef Teodor Konrad Nalecz Korzeniowski, and Herman Melville.

The Polish boat builder stimulated Johnnie's interest in the sea. He wondered where the man intended to sail once he finished his boat. Johnnie asked the man's sons, but they didn't know. They just shrugged their shoulders, sucked in their pudgy cheeks and blew snot from their dirt-covered noses straight to the ground. Since Johnnie's mother always snarled, "There he goes again," whenever she heard the hammering, he never discussed it with her.

One early-fall morning Johnnie was passing the Polish family's house and he stopped to look at the boat. It was out in the yard inverted on two homemade horses and was about thirty feet long. The man was planing the sides. He nodded to Johnnie and continued planing. His bald head was covered with sweat and he was humming a fast, foreign-sounding tune.

"Where are you going to sail her?" Johnnie asked him. The man stopped for a moment and stared blankly at Johnnie, as if he hadn't understood the question. Johnnie considered asking him again, but then thought that perhaps the man did not speak English very well, so he waited. Finally the man shrugged, gave a vague grunt, shoved his small pair of glasses up the bridge of his short, fat nose, they slid back down again, and he continued to plane. Johnnie watched him for a few minutes and then walked away.

The following spring the Polish family left town. The boat was moved on a flatbed truck, strapped down with heavy rope. The man and his two sons and the grandmother drove away in a car behind the truck. Johnnie couldn't remember who was driving the truck, but he recalled that when he went into his house and told his mother that the boat and the Polish family were gone, his mother said, "Thank Jesus, we won't have to listen to that awful poundin' no more."

ROAD KID

OUTSIDE BATON ROUGE, Sailor said to Lula, "Sweetheart, keep your panties up. We're in Jimmy Swaggart country."

Lula giggled. "Jimmy's just another of them cheapskate preachers? Wantin' somethin' for nothin', is how I see it."

"At Pee Dee I heard about a guy named Top Hat Robichaux lives around here. Real name's Clarence, I think, but he's from the town of Top Hat, which is just north a ways, so that's what they called him."

"What's he do?"

"Used to be a safecracker. Now he's got his own country church up in Top Hat, Louisiana. He started it at Pee Dee, called the Holy Roller Rebel Raiders."

"Sounds like a football team," said Lula. "*Two* football teams."

Sailor and Lula both laughed. They were buzzing west on Interstate 10 in the Bonneville with the top down. Sailor kept on right past the capital city but slowed to a stop a mile or so beyond the western boundary to pick up a hitchhiker.

"Sure you want to do this?" asked Lula. "Might be a way they could track us."

"He's just a kid, honey. Look at him."

The hitchhiker was a boy of about fifteen or sixteen

with a pack on his back, and he was carrying a large, covered cardboard box that he placed gently on the back seat next to him. His face was covered with freckles and acne. There wasn't a clear spot on it other than the whites of his eyes, which were a washed-out blue. His long brown hair was straggly, uncombed, and looked as if it hadn't been shampooed for weeks, if not months. He wore an old green army field jacket with the name MEN-DOZA sewn in capital letters on a white strip above the left breast pocket. The boy had an uneven smile on his face that exposed his jagged, yellow teeth.

"Thanks a lot," the boy said as he settled into the car, stowing his pack on the floor between his feet. "I been standin' out there off and on for two hours, ha-ha! Since noon about, ha-ha! Cops catch ya hitchin' on a interstate around here they throw ya on a county road crew for a week, 'less you can pay the ticket, ha-ha! Which I ain't got, ha-ha!"

"My name's Sailor, and this here's Lula. What's yours?"

"Marvin DeLoach," said the boy. "But ever'body calls me Roach, ha-ha! Roach DeLoach, ha-ha!"

"You always make that strange little funny laugh when you talk?" asked Lula.

"Ain't laughin', ha-ha!" said Roach.

"What you got in the box?" asked Sailor.

"My dogs, ha-ha!"

Roach slid the top off and tilted the box slightly toward the front. Inside were six small husky pups that couldn't have been more than two weeks old.

"I'm headed to Alaska, ha-ha!" said Roach. "These dogs is gonna be my sled team, ha-ha!"

"This kid's crazy," Lula said to Sailor.

"Where you from, Roach?" Sailor asked.

"If you mean where was I born, it was Belzoni,

Missi'ppi, ha-ha! But I been brought up in Baton Rouge."

"Why you goin' to Alaska?" said Lula. "And where'd you get them puppies? They look sick."

Roach stared down into the box at the baby huskies and stroked each of them twice with a religiously unwashed hand. The dogs whimpered and licked his dirty fingers.

"I saw this movie on the TV, ha-ha! *The Call of the Wild.* I ain't never seen snow, ha-ha! I got these dogs at the pound. Nobody wanted 'em, ha-ha! Ever'body here got theirself pit bulls or some kinda hounds. I'm gonna feed these boys good so they'll be big and powerful and they can pull me real fast through the snow, ha-ha!"

Roach pulled a piece of raw cow's liver out of one of the pockets of the field jacket and began ripping little bits off it and feeding them to the dogs.

"Sailor!" Lula screeched when she saw this. "Stop! Stop the car now!"

Sailor pulled off the road onto the shoulder of the highway and stopped. Lula opened her door and jumped out.

"I'm sorry, but I can't take this," she said. "Roach, or whatever your name is, you come out of there with them dogs this instant!"

Roach stuck the liver back in his pocket and pulled his pack and the box of tiny canines after him. Once he and his belongings were deposited on the roadside, Lula hopped back into the car and slammed the door.

"I'm truly sorry? I'm truly sorry, Roach," she said. "But you ain't gonna make it to Alaska? Least not any part of the way with us. You'd best find a party to take care of those dogs proper, before they all die? And, if you don't mind my sayin' so? You could most certainly use some serious lookin' after yourself, startin' with a bath! Bye!"

Lula took a pair of sunglasses off the dashboard and put them on.

"Drive," she said to Sailor.

Once they were rolling again, Sailor said to Lula, "You don't feel you was a little hard on the boy, honey?"

"I know you're thinkin' that I got more'n some of my mama in me? Well, I couldn't help it, Sailor, I really couldn't. I'm sorry for that boy, but when he pulled that drippin' hunk of awful-smellin' meat out of his pocket? I near barfed. And them poor diseased puppies!"

Sailor laughed. "Just part of life on the road, peanut."

"Do me a favor, Sailor? Don't pick up no more hitchers, okay?"

TALK PRETTY
TO ME

"KNOW WHAT I LIKE BEST, honey?" said Lula, as Sailor guided the Bonneville out of Lafayette toward Lake Charles.

"What's that, peanut?"

"When you talk pretty to me."

Sailor laughed. "That's easy enough. I mean, it don't come hard. Back at Pee Dee all I had to do to cheer myself up was think about you. Your big grey eyes, of course, but mostly your skinny legs."

"You think my legs is too skinny?"

"For some, maybe, but not for me they ain't."

"A girl ain't perfect, you know, except in them magazines."

"I been makin' do."

"Can't see where it's harmed you none."

"I ain't complainin', sweetheart, you know that."

"I think most men, if not all, is missin' an element, anyways."

"What's that mean?"

"Men got a kind of automatic shutoff valve in their head? Like, you're talkin' to one and just gettin' to the part where you're gonna say what you really been wantin' to say, and then you say it and you look at him and he ain't even heard it. Not like it's too complicated or

73

somethin', just he ain't about to really listen. One might lie sometime and tell ya he knows just what you mean, but I ain't buyin'. 'Cause later you say somethin' else he woulda got if he'd understood you in the first place, only he don't, and you know you been talkin' for no good reason. It's frustratin'."

"You think I been lyin' to you, Lula?"

Lula stayed quiet for a full minute, listening to the heavy hum of the V-8.

"Lula? You there?"

"Yeah, I'm here."

"You upset with me?"

"No, Sailor, darlin', I ain't upset. Just it's shockin' sometimes when what you think turns out to not be what you think at all."

"It's why I don't think no more'n necessary."

"You know, I had this awful, long dream last night? Tell me what you think of it. I'm out walkin' and I come to this field. This is all in bright color? And there's all these bodies of dead horses and dead children lyin' all around. I'm sad, but I'm not really sad. It's like I know they're all gone to a better place. Then a old woman comes up to me and tells me I got to bleed the bodies so they can be made into mummies. She shows me how to make a cut at the sides of the mouths of the corpses to drain 'em. Then I'm supposed to carry the bodies over a bridge across a real beautiful river into an old barn.

"Everything's really peaceful and lovely where I am, with green grass and big trees at the edge of the field. I'm not sure I got the strength to drag the bodies of the horses all that way. I'm frightened but I'm ready to do it anyway. And I'm sorta cryin' but not really sad? I can't explain the feelin' exactly. So I walk to the rear of this huge grey horse. I go around to his mouth and start to cut him. As soon as I touch him with the knife he wakes up and attacks me. The horse is furious. He gets up and chases me across the bridge and into and through the old barn. Then I woke up. You were sleepin' hard. And I just laid there and thought about how even if you love someone it isn't always possible to have it change your life."

"I don't know what your dream means, sweetheart," said Sailor, "but once I heard my mama ask my daddy if he loved her. They were yellin' at each other, like usual, and he told her the only thing he ever loved was the movie *Bad Men of Missouri,* which he said he seen sixteen times."

"What I mean about men," said Lula.

SURVIVORS

"NO, MARIETTA, I haven't found 'em."

"Maybe they ain't *in* N.O., Johnnie. They could be dead in a ditch in Pascagoula, Missi'ppi, by now. Or possibly Lula's barefoot and pregnant in Pine Bluff, Arkansas, and that horrible Sailor person's pumpin' gas in a fillin' station for two dollars an hour."

"Calm down, Marietta. If there'd been an accident we woulda known about it by now. There ain't no use your gettin' exercised prematurely."

"Prematurely! Don't toss feathers at me, Johnnie Farragut. My only child been kidnapped by a dangerous criminal and you keep tellin' me to be calm!"

"I'll handle it, Marietta. Like I told you, there ain't no evidence Lula done nothin' against her will."

"Well, you better get a move on, Johnnie, before that boy got her holdin' down a Memphis street corner and shootin' dope up her arms."

"Really, Marietta, you got more scenarios swimmin' around in your brain than Carter got pills. Try to take it easy. Go over to Myrtle Beach for a few days."

"I'm stayin' right here by the phone until you find Lula, then I'm comin' to get her."

"Just hold tight, woman. I'll call you again in a couple days whether I got a lead or not."

"You just got to locate Lula, Johnnie. This is the kinda mistake can take a Hindu's lifetime to unfix. I got to attend a meetin' of the Daughters of the Confederacy from two to four tomorrow afternoon, otherwise I'll be at home. You call soon's you got somethin', even if it's three in the A.M."

"I will, Marietta. Goodbye now."

Johnnie hung up and sat in the telephone booth, thinking about Marietta Pace Fortune. She was still a good-looking woman but she was getting more peculiar than ever. Marietta had always been nervous and demanding. Why he was still sweet on her after all these years Johnnie couldn't quite figure. Marrying her was out of the question, it just wasn't something Marietta would do. She wasn't cut out for a December romance, she said. The woman wouldn't be fifty for two or three years yet and she acted like life forgot her address. Except when it came to Lula, that is.

At the far end of Inez's Fais-Dodo Bar on Toulouse Street, Reginald San Pedro Sula, wearing his porkpie hat and a green seersucker leisure suit, sat on a stool drinking a martini. He spotted Johnnie walking toward the door.

"*Hola!* Señor Farragut!" Reggie shouted. "We meet again."

Johnnie went over to Reggie and shook hands.

"I thought you were in Austin, Texas. Or Takes-us, as they say in these parts."

"I was. Now I am on my way back to Utila, in the morning. Would you like to enjoy a martini with me?"

"Why not?" said Johnnie, hoisting himself onto the stool to Reggie's right. "How was the fishin'?"

"I think they are too serious, these American fishermen. In Honduras we are not so concerned with the method."

Reggie ordered a martini for Johnnie and another for himself.

"So," said Johnnie, "it's back to the islands."

"Yes. I spoke yesterday to my son, Archibald Leach San Pedro Sula, who is named after Cary Grant, and he told me there was a shooting. Teddy Roosevelt, one of the local shrimp boat captains, was on a picnic with King George Blanco and King George's wife, Colombia, and there was, apparently, a disagreement of some kind, during which King George and Colombia were killed. Teddy Roosevelt is in jail now. These people are all friends of mine, so I must return and find out what happened."

"This island of yours sounds like a kind of unpredictable place."

Reggie laughed. "It has its moments of uncertainty. But how are you finding New Orleans, Señor Farragut?"

"Call me Johnnie. N.O. always been a good town to sit around in."

"I can tell you are an intelligent man, Johnnie. One difference between your country and mine is that in the islands it does not pay to reveal one's intelligence. I am reminded of the time I saw a blue heron walking next to a river. He looked like a Chinese gentleman in a blue coat wobbling along the rocks. He appeared extremely vulnerable and defenseless, yet he was undoubtedly a survivor. That is our duty, Johnnie, as intelligent men, to survive."

Reggie raised his glass to Johnnie's. *"Hasta siempre,"* he said.

"Hasta siempre," said Johnnie.

"Do you know how it came about that copper wire was invented in Scotland?" Reggie asked.

"How's that?"

"Two Scotsmen were fighting over a penny."

Johnnie finished off his martini.

"I got to admit, Reggie," he said, sliding off the stool, "you're one in a dozen."

OLD NOISE

"YOU DIDN'T RAISE A FOOL, Marietta. Lula got too much Pace in her to throw her life away on trash. My guess is she's havin' herself a time, is all."

Marietta and Dalceda Delahoussaye were sitting on the side porch of Marietta's house drinking Martini & Rossi sweet vermouth over crushed ice with a lemon slice. Dalceda had been best friends with Marietta for close to thirty years, ever since they boarded together at Miss Cook's School in Beaufort. They'd never lived further apart in that period than a ten-minute walk.

"Remember Vernon Landis? The man owned a Hispano-Suiza he kept in Royce Womble's garage all those years before he sold it for twenty-five thousand dollars to the movie company in Wilmington? His wife, Althea, ran off with a wholesale butcher from Hayti, Missouri. The man gave her a diamond ring big enough to stuff a turkey and guess what? She was back with Vernon in six weeks."

"Dal? Just *what,* you tell me, has Althea Landis's inability to control herself have to do with my baby Lula's bein' stole by this awful demented man?"

"Marietta! Sailor Ripley prob'ly ain't no more or less demented than anyone we know."

"Oh, Dal, he's lowlife. He's what we been avoidin' all our lives, and now my only child's at his mercy."

"You always been one to panic, Marietta. When Enos Dodge didn't ask you right off to go with him to the Beau Regard Country Club cotillion in 1959, you panicked. Threatened to kill yourself or accept an invitation from Biff Bethune. And what happened? Enos Dodge'd been in Fayetteville with his daddy and asked you soon as he got back two days later. This ain't a moment to panic, lovey. You're gonna have to quit spittin' and ride it on out."

"You're always such a comfort to me, Dal."

"I give you what you need, is all. A talkin'-to."

"What I need is Lula safe at home."

"Safe? Safe? Ain't that a stitch! Ain't nobody nowhere never been safe a second of their life."

Dalceda drained the last drop of vermouth from her glass.

"You got any more of this red vinegar in the house?" she asked.

Marietta rose and went into the pantry and came out carrying a sealed bottle. She unscrewed the cap and poured Dalceda a drink and freshened her own before sitting back down.

"And what about you?" said Dalceda.

"What about me?"

"When's the last time you been out with a man? Let alone been to bed with one."

Marietta clucked her tongue twice before answering.

"I plain ain't interested," she said, and took a long sip from her glass.

Dalceda laughed. "What was it you used to tell me about how Clyde carried on when you and him made love? About his gruntin' that come from way down inside sounded so ancient? Old noise, you called it. Told me you felt like you was bein' devoured by a unstoppable beast, and it was the most thrillin' thing ever happened to you."

"Dal, I swear I hate talkin' to you. You remember too much."

"Hate hearin' the truth is what it is. You're just shit scared Lula feels the same way about Sailor as you did with Clyde."

"Oh, Dal, how could she? I mean, do you think she does? This Sailor ain't nothin' like Clyde."

"How do you know, Marietta? You ever tried the boy on for size?"

Dalceda laughed. Marietta drank.

"And Mr. Dogface Farragut comes mopin' and sniffin' around you regular," said Dalceda. "You could start with him. Or how about that old gangster, Marcello 'Crazy Eyes' Santos, used to proposition you when you was married to Clyde?"

Marietta snorted. "He stopped askin' after Clyde died. My bein' too available musta thrown him off the scent."

"That's most certainly the case with Louis Delahoussaye the Third," said Dalceda. "I don't think he's asked for it more'n twice in six months for a grand total of a not so grand eight and one-half minutes."

"Dal? You think I oughta keep dyein' my hair or let it go white?"

"Marietta, what I think is we both need another drink."

NIGHT LIFE

"I WOULDN'T MIND A LITTLE NIGHT LIFE," said Lula. "How about you?"

Sailor cruised the Bonneville slowly along Napoleon Avenue, casing the neighborhood. It was nine o'clock at night and they were in the town of Nuñez, on the Louisiana side of the Louisiana-Texas border.

"Hard to tell what's shakin' in a place like this, honey," said Sailor. "You don't want to be walkin' in the wrong door."

"Maybe there's a place we could hear some music. I feel like dancin'. We could ask somewhere," Lula said.

Sailor turned left into Lafitte Road and spotted a Red Devil gas station that still had its lights on.

"Someone up here might know somethin'," he said, and pulled the car over.

A skinny, pimply-faced guy of about eighteen, wearing dirty yellow coveralls and a crumpled black baseball cap with a red felt N on it, walked over to them.

"Gas?" he said.

"Got enough, thanks," said Sailor. "We're lookin' for a place has some music, where we can maybe get somethin' to eat, too. Anything like that around here?"

"Cornbread's," said the attendant. "They got western. No food, though, 'cept bar nibbles."

Lula slid over in the front seat and leaned across Sailor.

"How about rock 'n' roll?" she asked.

"There's a boogie joint just about a mile straight out Lafitte here. But that's a black place mostly."

"What's the name of it?" asked Sailor.

"Club Zanzibar."

"You say it's straight ahead a mile?"

"About. Where Lafitte crosses over Galvez Highway. State Road 86."

"Thanks," said Sailor.

The Club Zanzibar was in a white wood building on the left-hand side of the road. A string of multicolored lights was hung over the front. Sailor parked the Bonneville across from the club and cut the engine.

"You ready for this?" he asked.

"We'll find out in a hurry," said Lula.

When they walked in, a band was playing a slow blues and three or four couples were swaying on the dance floor. There were a dozen tables and a long bar in the room. Eight of the tables were occupied and six or seven men sat or stood at the bar. Everyone in the place was black except for one white woman, who was sitting alone at a table smoking a cigarette and drinking Pearl straight from the bottle.

"Come on," said Lula, taking Sailor by the hand and leading him onto the dance floor.

The tune was John Lee Hooker's "Sugar Mama," and Lula insinuated her body into Sailor's and left it there. After that the band picked up the beat. Sailor and Lula danced for twenty minutes before Sailor begged off and dragged Lula over to the bar and ordered two Lone Star beers. The bartender, a tall, heavyset man in his early fifties, served the beers, took Sailor's money and gave him his change with a big smile.

"This is a friendly place, son," said the bartender. "You folks just relax and have a nice time."

"No problem," said Lula. "You got a real fine band here."

The bartender smiled again and moved on down the bar.

"You notice that woman when we come in?" Lula said to Sailor. "The white woman sittin' by herself?"

"Uh huh," said Sailor.

"Well, she ain't talked to nobody and ain't nobody spoke to her that I could tell. What you make of that?"

"Honey, we bein' strangers here and all, this is the kinda place we don't want to make nothin' of nothin'."

"You think she's pretty?"

Sailor looked at the woman. She lit a new cigarette off a butt, then squashed the butt in an ashtray. She was thirty years old, maybe more. Shoulder-length bleached blond hair, black at the roots. Clear skin, green eyes. Long, straight nose with a small bump on it. She was wearing a low-cut lavender dress that would have emphasized her breasts had she not been so flat chested. Slender.

"I tend to like 'em with a little more meat on the bones," said Sailor. "Face ain't bad, though."

Lula got quiet and sucked on her beer bottle.

"What's wrong, sweetheart? Somethin' botherin' you?"

"Aw, it's just Mama. I been thinkin' about her. She's prob'ly worried to death by now."

"More than likely."

"I want to call her and tell her I'm okay. That *we're* okay."

"I ain't so sure it's a great idea, but that's up to you. Just don't tell her where we are."

"Pardon me?" Lula said to the bartender. "Y'all got a phone here I can use?"

"Straight back by the gents'."

"Back in a bit," she said to Sailor, and kissed him on the nose.

Marietta answered the telephone on the second ring.

"I have a collect call from Lula Fortune," said the operator. "Will you accept?"

"Of course!" said Marietta. "Lula? Where *are* you? You all right?"

"I'm fine, Mama. I just wanted to tell you not to worry."

"Why, how *could* I not worry? Not knowin' what's happenin' to you or where you are? Are you with that boy?"

"If you mean Sailor, Mama, yes I am."

"Are you comin' home soon, Lula? I need you here."

"Need me for what, Mama? I'm perfectly fine, and safe, too."

"You in a dance hall or somethin'? I can hear music behind you."

"Just a place."

"Really, Lula, this ain't right!"

"Right?! Mama, was it right for you to sic Johnnie Farragut on us? How could you *do* that?"

"Did you run into Johnnie in New Orleans? Lula, are you in New Orleans?"

"No, Mama, I'm in Mexico, and we're about to get on a airplane to Argentina!"

"Argentina! Lula, you're outa your mind. Now you just tell me where you are and I'll come for you. I won't say nothin' to the police about Sailor, I promise. He can do what he wants, I don't care."

"Mama, I'm hangin' up this phone now."

"No, baby, don't! Can I send you somethin'? You runnin' low on money? I'll wire you some money if you tell me where you are."

"I ain't that dumb, Mama. Sailor and I been on a crime spree? Knockin' off convenience stores all across the South? Ain't you read about it?"

Marietta was crying. "Lula? I love you, baby. I just want you to be all right."

"I am all right, Mama. That's why I called, to let you know. I gotta go."

"Call me again soon? I'll be waitin' by the phone."

"Don't be crazy, Mama. Take care of yourself."

Lula hung up.

Sailor and the bleached blond in the lavender dress were together on the dance floor. Lula saw them, went over to the bar, picked up a beer bottle and threw it at Sailor. The bottle bounced off his back and clanged to the floor, bouncing but not breaking. He turned around and looked at Lula. Nobody else in the place gave any sign that they'd seen what had happened. Lula ran out.

Sailor found her sitting on the ground, leaning against the passenger side of the Bonneville. Lula's eyes were red and wet but she wasn't crying. Sailor knelt down next to her.

"I was just wastin' time, peanut, till you come back."

"It's me who's wastin' time, Sailor, bein' with you."

"Honey, I'm sorry. It wasn't nothin'. Come on and get up and we'll take off."

"Leave me be for a minute? Mama gets all insane and then I see you dancin' with some oil town tramp. How you figure I'm gonna feel?"

"Told you not to call her."

Sailor stood and leaned against the hood of the car until Lula got up and climbed inside. He got in and started it up. Lula took Sailor's blue canvas jacket from the back seat and put it on. She kissed Sailor on the cheek, put her head down sideways on his lap and went to sleep. Sailor drove.

LATE BLUES

"JOHNNIE! AT LAST! I thought you was never gonna call."

"I got some news, Marietta. Lula and Sailor been here. They checked out of the Hotel Brazil on Frenchmen Street two days ago."

"Listen, Johnnie, Lula called me last night. She knew you were in N.O., so they left the city."

"Did she tell you where she was callin' from?"

"No, but my guess is they're headed west, so prob'ly Texas. Could be Houston. Their money must be runnin' low. I don't think Sailor had much to begin with, if any, and Lula took the six hundred she had saved in the Cherokee Thrift."

"How'd she sound? Was she doin' okay?"

"How could she be doin' okay, Johnnie? She's tryin' to prove somethin' to me, that's all. Lula ain't doin' no more'n showin' off, defyin' me."

"Marietta, she's tryin' to grow up, is all. It don't have everything to do with you. I don't mean to insult you or nothin', but Lula got to get shut of you somehow, and this is how she's chose to do it. I understand how painful it is for you."

"How *could* you understand? She's the only flesh and blood I got left I care anything about. Lula's my *daughter*, Johnnie. I'm comin' to New Orleans."

"Hold on, Marietta. There ain't no good you can do here until I get a line on which way they went. Could be they're halfway to Chicago."

"They're headed west, Johnnie, I know it. Prob'ly to California. Lula always has wanted to go there. I'll be in on the Piedmont flight at seven tomorrow night. Meet me at the airport and we can get goin' right away."

"I'll meet you, Marietta, if that's what you want, but I'm against it."

"Seven tomorrow evenin'. We can eat at Galatoire's. Fix it."

Marietta hung up.

Johnnie hung up the hotel phone and walked out onto the balcony overhanging Barracks Street. It was one in the morning and the air was warm but misty. He could hear a recording of Babs Gonzales singing "Ornithology" in his froggy voice coming from a radio or stereo. "All the cats are standin' on the corner," Babs Gonzales sang, "waitin' for the chicks to finish their slave." Johnnie lit up a Hoyo de Monterrey cigar and tossed the match into the street.

In 1950, Elia Kazan had filmed *Panic in the Streets* here, staging a shooting on the Barracks Street Wharf. Johnnie had read somewhere that it was the actor Jack Palance's first movie. Palance, with his face resculpted following a car wreck into a wicked Mongol mask, portrayed Blackie, the perfect, unrepentant killer. Palance could convey cruelty more convincingly than anyone in those days, Johnnie thought. It takes a certain amount of desperation to do that. "I'm not a desperate person," Johnnie said aloud. He blew smoke from his cigar into the night mist. If a man is no good at convincing himself of something, he thought, then there isn't much chance he'll do a very good job of convincing anyone else.

"Ornithology" segued into King Pleasure and Betty Carter's "Little Red Top." "You really got me spinning," they sang. Johnnie stayed on the balcony until the song ended before he went back inside. He had an idea for a story about a man with a terrible disease that robs him of his ability to remember anything unless he mutilates himself.

DAL'S SECRET

"DAL? I'M GOIN' TO N.O."

"You hear somethin' from Johnnie?"

"Just that they left the hotel they was stayin' in. Fire-trap called the Brazil? Johnnie don't know no more."

"Marietta, I'm dead against it. Leave Lula be. It'll take years to undo what you're doin'."

"I can't help it, Dal. I can't just sit around waitin'."

"I might as well tell you now about Clyde."

"What *about* Clyde?"

"One time he come to me."

"One time he come to you? Dal, did you and him have an affair?"

"Not nearly. No, he come to ask me about you. Before Lula was born."

"What *about* me?"

"Thought maybe you was too high-strung to have children, and wanted my opinion."

"Go on."

"Told him I thought it was a good idea, your havin' a child. That he shouldn't fret."

"Swell of you, Dal. How come you never told me before?"

"Clyde asked me not to."

"Clyde been dead for years."

"I promised him, Marietta."

"So why confess now?"

"It ain't a confession."

"Why bring it up then?"

" 'Cause I think you're makin' a mistake, what you're doin' now. Clyde wouldn't want it."

"Clyde ain't gonna know about it, Dalceda. Unless you got some way of communicatin' with him I ain't heard about."

"You have a safe trip, Marietta. If you need me to do somethin' for you here, give a shout. And give my love to Lula, if you find her."

"Dal, I know you think I'm wrong on this, but I mean well."

"I know you do, Marietta. Bye."

"Bye, Dal."

After she hung up, Marietta started to cry. She cried for a full ten minutes, until the phone rang. By the fourth ring Marietta had composed herself sufficiently to pick it up.

"Marietta? It's Dal. You stop cryin' yet?"

"Just now. Almost."

"Stop it now, hear? Pull yourself together and go do what you have to. Maybe I'm the one is wrong."

"You ain't wrong, Dal. Not for you, anyway. You're the only one knows me."

"Love you, Marietta."

"Love you, Dal."

"Bye again."

"Bye."

BAD IDEAS

"SOMETIMES I FEEL just like one of Dracula's wives. You know, those skinny women in see-through robes with long hair and fingernails who follow the Count around and do what he says?"

Lula was sitting on the edge of the motel bed filing her nails while Sailor did his daily fifty fingertip push-ups.

"Sure," said Sailor, "I seen the movie. But why?"

"I get so low down. It's as if someone's sucked all the blood out of my body."

"We all get that way once in a while, honey," Sailor said between push-ups. "As my grandaddy used to say, ain't no one person got a monopoly on grief."

"Oh, I know," said Lula. "I'm not even feelin' particularly sorry for myself. It's just I'd like it sometime that Daddy hadn't died on me so soon? And that Mama wasn't such a crazy bitch more'n twice a month? And that she didn't hold it against you about havin' to kill Bob Ray Lemon? Lots and lots."

Sailor finished the last of his fingertips and sat up with his back against the bed.

"My grandaddy used to read the obituaries every Friday mornin' at breakfast," Sailor said. "He'd get the newspaper and commence to tell me who died and what of and all about their lives and relatives left behind. Grandaddy'd shake his head and laugh and wonder about why poor departed Cleve Sumpter married his first wife,

Irma Sykes, had three children and went into the milli-
nery business in Aiken, divorced Irma, got hitched to
Edna Mae Raley, quit makin' hats, opened up a barbecue
restaurant in McCall, and twenty years later died of em-
physema while listenin' to the Braves ball game on the
front porch of a old-people's home in Asheville.''

"Sounds morbid to me," said Lula. "Readin' the obits?
I never look at 'em. And why'd he do it just on Fridays?"

"I don't know," said Sailor. "But I enjoyed listenin' to
Grandaddy talk about the people as if he knew each and
every one of 'em personal."

"What'd they write about your grandaddy when he
died?" asked Lula. "Or is he still livin'?"

"He died when I was up at Pee Dee," Sailor said.
"They wouldn't let me out to go to the funeral, of course.
Grandaddy was my best friend when I was a kid. Family
give him some shit, I guess, 'cause he wasn't no great
shakes in business, and he done some hard time early on
for assaultin' an officer when he was in the service. I never
read his obituary notice, if there was one, but that's fair
enough. Prob'ly they didn't have much in there about his
teachin' me to hunt and fish or cook biscuits."

"Sailor?"

"Yeah?"

"Wouldn't it be fabulous if we someway stayed in love
for the rest of our lives?"

Sailor laughed. "You think of the weirdest damn
things to say sometimes, peanut. Ain't we been doin' a
pretty fair job this far?"

Lula reached down with both of her arms and put them
around Sailor's neck. She dropped her emery board on
the floor.

"Oh, you know what I mean, don't you, honey? It'd
make everything so simple."

"At Pee Dee all you think about is the future, you

know?" said Sailor. "Gettin' out? And what you'll do
when you're on the outside again. But I'm out now and I
don't know what to think about yet."

"I just think about things as they come up," said Lula.
"I never been much of a planner."

"It ain't altogether terrible just to let things go along
sometimes," Sailor said. "My grandaddy once read me
the obituary of a man who'd owned a big manufacturin'
company of some kind and run for U.S. senator four
times and lost every time. 'Imagine all them bastards that
man had to pretend to like,' Grandaddy said, 'and all for
nothin'.' I ain't gonna do nothin' for no good reason,
Lula. All I know for sure is there's already more'n a few
bad ideas runnin' around loose out there."

Lula reached over and turned on the radio that was on
the table next to the bed.

"If I could but win your heart, little girl, then I would
have treasure untold." It was Jimmie Rodgers, the Singing Brakeman.

"I love these old yodelly country songs," said Lula.
"They're all so corny but sweet, too."

Sailor nodded. "My grandaddy told me that when
Jimmie Rodgers died, he went down to the depot to
watch the train that was carryin' his body back to Merid-
ian, Mississippi, go by. Jimmie had the TB so bad they
kept a cot in the recordin' studio so that he could lay
down and rest after doin' a tune."

"Musta been a lot of people loved him," said Lula.
"That must be a great feelin'. To know there's all these
strangers out there think so much of you?"

"My experience, the more people get to know each
other the less they get along," said Sailor. "It's best to
keep people to bein' strangers. That way they don't get
disappointed so easy."

HARD NEWS

"HOW MUCH WE GOT LEFT, honey?"

"Under a hundred," said Sailor.

Sailor and Lula were in a Shell station in Houston. Sailor had just filled the Bonneville with regular and checked the oil and water.

"You want to stick around here, Sailor? See if we can get some work?"

"Not in Houston. This is where they'd expect us to stop. We'll be better off in some place more out of the way."

"You want me to drive for a stretch? Give you a chance to rest."

"That'd be good, Lula."

Sailor kissed her and climbed into the back seat and lay down. Lula slid behind the wheel and lit up a More. She wheeled the car back into traffic and toward the entrance to the interstate, following the loop around Houston headed for San Antonio. She clicked on the radio. Perez Prado's band, playing "Cherry Pink and Apple Blossom White," came on. "Another damn oldies station," Lula muttered, and turned the dial. She found a nationwide call-in talk show and left it there.

"Come in, Montgomery, Alabama," said the host, a man with a gruff Brooklyn accent.

"Artie? That you, Artie?" said the caller, an elderly-sounding woman.

"Yes, ma'am. What's on your almost-perfect mind this evening?"

"How ya feelin', Artie? I heard you wasn't doin' too well recent."

"I'm fine, thank you. I had a cardiac infarction but I'm on a new diet and exercising regularly. I've never felt better."

"Well, that's so good to hear, Artie. You know some of us depend on you down this way. You're so entertainin' and you get so many interestin' guests."

"Thank you. It's listeners such as yourself who made me want to get up out of that hospital bed and back into the studio as fast as I could."

"Just remember, Artie, it's the Good Lord you got to thank for everything. He's watchin' over us."

"Thanks for the call, ma'am. San Francisco, California, hello."

"Hello, Artie? This is Manny Wolf in San Francisco."

"Mark Twain said the coldest winter he ever spent was a summer in San Francisco. How you doin', Manny?"

"Oh, pretty good, Artie. Heard you had a heart attack."

"Yeah, but I'm okay now."

"Well, Bill Beaumont did a bang-up job while you were out."

"He's number one, isn't he? What's on your almost-perfect mind tonight, Manny?"

"The Giants, Artie. They sure did a nosedive, didn't they?"

"Injuries, Manny. You can't win ball games if half the pitching staff goes down, including three starters. I look for 'em to be back in it next year."

"They coulda made some deals, Artie."

"With what? Nobody wants damaged goods."

"They coulda made some deals they woulda tried."

"Wait till next year. Thanks for callin', Manny. Boston, Massachusetts, you're on the air with Artie Mayer."

"Jesus!" said Lula, attacking the dial. "How can anyone listen to this crap?"

She settled on an all-news station. Sailor was snoring. Lula took a last puff of her More and tossed it out the window.

"An alleged child prostitution ring that provided young girls for businessmen in Houston, Dallas, Fort Worth and other cities has been broken up by Houston police," said the radio. "Investigators theorized that the ring, which operated out of a redbrick warehouse building on the north side of downtown Houston near Buffalo Bayou, may be part of a larger operation run out of Los Angeles and New Orleans by Vietnamese citizens."

"Wow, this is good," said Lula. She turned up the volume.

"The ring's activities were revealed yesterday after a fifty-five-year-old Houston pai-gow dealer was arrested for allegedly having sex with a twelve-year-old girl at an Airport Loop motel Tuesday night. Chick Go, who works at Lucky Guy's card parlor, was apprehended in a raid on the Nighty-Night Motel. He was arraigned yesterday on charges of engaging in sex acts with a child and contributing to the delinquency of a minor. He was released on ten thousand dollars' bail. More arrests are expected.

"The young prostitutes' customers, said a police spokesman, were carefully selected, primarily successful businessmen who had something to lose if they ever informed authorities about the child sex ring. Most of the prostitutes are apparently runaways who need a place to live in exchange for sexual favors. Police said they have identified and questioned at least four girls, all Asians twelve to fifteen years old, who have been living in the North Houston warehouse with a Vietnamese pimp since February. The girls are being treated as victims, said police sergeant Amos Milburn. 'These are really just children,' he said, 'but they've been exposed to a lot already.' "

"I'll bet," said Lula, lighting up another cigarette.

"In international news, India plans to release crocodiles in the Ganges, the holy Hindu river in which millions of people bathe annually, to scavenge for corpses, authorities said. One hundred fifty crocodiles reared at a state-owned farm in southern Kerala state will be dumped in the river near cities where corpse pollution levels are the highest. The reptiles were supposed to be of a docile species, said a senior government official, but it seems the breeders bungled and reared attack crocodiles."

"Damn!" said Lula.

"The Indian official who supplied this information did so only on condition of anonymity. The *Crocodilus palustris* species, he said, has a reputation for killing and breeding quickly. Some one hundred thousand corpses are cremated on the banks of the Ganges in Varanasi every year, while millions of Hindus bathe in the river in the belief that the water will purify the soul and absolve them of sins. The government plans to cleanse the Ganges first at Varanasi, the holiest Hindu city. The Uttar Pradesh state authorities last October released five hundred turtles in the Ganges near Varanasi to try and reduce human pollution and now plan to put in the crocodiles to devour floating corpses dumped by Hindus too poor to pay for cremation."

"Holy shit!" said Lula. "It's the night of the livin' fuckin' dead!"

"What's that, peanut?" said Sailor, kissing her on the ear from behind.

"I can't take no more of this radio," she said, and switched it off. "I ain't never heard so much concentrated weirdness in my life. I know the news ain't always accurate, but the world's gettin' worse, I think, Sailor. And it don't sound like there's much we can do about it, neither."

"This ain't news, sweetheart. I hate to tell ya."

DON'T DIE
FOR ME

JOHNNIE CHEWED HIS TROUT slowly and care-fully. He was listening to Marietta while trying to avoid swallowing the bones.

"She's all I have, Johnnie. If I didn't go after Lula now, I'd never forgive myself."

"I understand how you feel, Marietta, it's just I can't see you're helpin' matters. Lula ain't a baby, she got a mind of her own. There comes a point you gotta let go."

Marietta put down her knife and fork, sat back in her chair and stared hard at Johnnie.

"You sound like some textbook on child rearin'," she said, "which is interestin', considerin' you never raised no children."

They sat in silence throughout the rest of their meal, and Marietta paid the check with cash, since Galatoire's did not accept credit cards.

Once they were outside on Bourbon Street, Johnnie said, "You want to spend the night in town or get on the road? Either way's solid with me."

"I can sleep in the car," said Marietta. "Let's head for Houston and see if we can pick up the trail."

Marietta settled back in the front passenger seat of Johnnie's 1987 candy-apple-red Cadillac Seville. She closed her eyes and thought about what Dalceda

Delahoussaye had said about Clyde's coming to her with his worry over Marietta's nervous nature. She'd done a good job, she thought, raising Lula. This situation with the Ripley boy was just a freak occurrence, something Marietta knew she could talk Lula out of face-to-face. She prayed that Lula wasn't pregnant again.

As soon as Johnnie was certain that Marietta had fallen asleep, he rolled down his window partway and lit up a Hoyo. He had committed himself to her, so he'd stick with the chase, but he didn't like the feel of it now. He had a foreboding about the whole deal. Johnnie kept the Cadillac at a steady seventy-five. Marietta's head was tilted back and to the side away from him. Her mouth was half open and her chest was rising and falling in a regular rhythm. He turned on the radio, keeping the sound low.

"Finally, a sad item in the sports news," said the radio. "Eligio Sardinias, a leading boxer in the 1930s who fought under the name Kid Chocolate, died today in Havana, the Cuban state radio reported. He was seventy-eight years old. The Cuban-born boxer was elected to the Boxing Hall of Fame in 1959. As Kid Chocolate, he won the world junior lightweight title in 1931, and followed that up by winning the New York featherweight title, then considered a major championship, in 1932, by beating Lew Feldman with a twelfth-round knockout. He fought for the world featherweight title in 1930, losing a fifteen-round decision to Battling Battalino. The next year he lost a bid for the world lightweight title against Tony Canzoneri, also in a fifteen-round decision. Kid Chocolate's professional record was a hundred thirty-two wins, ten losses and six draws, with fifty KOs."

Lew Feldman, thought Johnnie, must have been a Jewish fighter. There were lots of them in the old days. Barney Ross, of course, and Benny Leonard, both champions. Many who fought under Irish or Italian names. Maybe there was a story in this, Johnnie thought. A Jewish kid, just off the boat before the war, goes into the army, where he learns how to box from an old sergeant whose own pro career was cut short due to an injury. The kid takes the sergeant's name, Jack O'Leary. He fights his way close to the top, only to be prevented from getting a shot at the title by an anti-Semitic promoter who finds out the kid's a Jew.

The kid can win the title and the promoter knows it. The only way he'll let the kid in the ring, however, is if the kid agrees to take a dive so the promoter and his mob cronies can make a bundle betting against him. A real 1940s-style melodrama, Johnnie thought. Sergeant O'Leary is on his deathbed, wounded and dying. He gets wind of the tank job and sends word to the kid before the fight to win the title for him, to not disgrace the name Jack O'Leary. John Garfield could have played the kid in the movie, with Harry Carey as the sergeant, Eduardo Ciannelli as the crooked promoter, Arthur Kennedy as the kid's manager-trainer, Juano Hernandez as the corner man, and Priscilla Lane as the girlfriend.

Johnnie ran the movie over and over in his mind as he drove, reinventing the scenes. The title would be *Don't Die for Me*. Nothing in real life, thought Johnnie, ever seemed quite as honest as this.

THE MIDDLE
OF THINGS

IN SAN ANTONIO, Lula said, "You know about the
Alamo?"

"Talked about it in school, I remember," said Sailor.
"And I seen the old John Wayne movie where mostly
nothin' happens till the Mexicans overrun the place."

Sailor and Lula were in La Estrella Negra eating birria
con arroz y frijoles and drinking Tecate with wedges of
lime.

"Guess it's a pretty big deal here," said Lula. "Noticed
drivin' in how ever'thing's named after it. Alamo Road,
Alamo Street, Alamo Square, Alamo Buildin', Hotel Alamo. They ain't forgettin' it in a hurry."

"Pretty place, though, San Antone," said Sailor.

"So what we gonna do, hon? About money, I mean."

"I ain't worried. Figure we'll stop somewhere between
here and El Paso and find some work."

"When you was a boy?"

"Uh huh."

"What'd you think about doin' when you grew up?"

"Pilot. Always wanted to be a airline pilot."

"Like for TWA or Delta, you mean?"

"Yeah. Thought that'd be cool, you know, wearin' a
captain's hat and takin' them big birds up over the ocean.
Hang out with stews in Rome and L.A."

"Why didn't you do it?"

Sailor laughed. "Never really got the chance, did I? Wasn't nobody about to help me toward it, you know? Not bein' much of a student, always gettin' in trouble one way or another, I kinda lost sight of it."

"You coulda joined the air force, learned to fly."

"Tried once. They didn't want me 'cause of my record. Too many scrapes. I never even been in a plane."

"Shoot, Sail, we oughta take a long flight when we got some money to waste. Fly to Paris."

"I'd go for that."

As soon as they'd finished eating, Sailor said, "Let's keep movin', Lula. Big towns is where they'll look."

Sailor drove with Lula curled up on the seat next to him. Patsy Cline was on the radio, singing "I Fall to Pieces."

"I wish I'd been born when Patsy Cline was singin'," said Lula.

"What's the difference?" Sailor asked. "You can still listen to her records."

"I coulda seen her maybe. She got the biggest voice? Like if Aretha Franklin woulda been a country singer all those years ago. That's what I always wanted to do, Sailor, be a singer. I ever tell you that?"

"Not that I recall."

"When I was little, eight or nine? Mama took me to Charlotte and put me in a talent show. It was at a big movie theater, and there was all these kids lined up on the stage. Each of us had to perform when our name was called. Kids tap-danced, played instruments or sang, mostly. One boy did magic tricks. Another boy juggled balls and stood on his head while he whistled 'Dixie' or somethin'."

"What'd you do?"

"Sang 'Stand By Your Man,' the Tammy Wynette tune? Mama thought it'd be extra cute, havin' me sing such a grown-up number."

"How'd it go?"

"Not too bad. Course I couldn't hit most of the high notes, and all the other kids on stage was talkin' and makin' noises durin' my turn."

"You win?"

"No. Some boy played 'Stars Fell on Alabama' on a harmonica did."

"Why'd you quit singin'?"

"Mama decided I didn't have no talent. Said she didn't wanta waste no more money on lessons. This was when I was thirteen? Prob'ly she was right. No sense playin' at it. You got a voice like Patsy's, you ain't got no hesitation about where you're headed."

"Ain't easy when you're kinda in the middle of things," said Sailor.

"Like us, you mean," said Lula. "That's where we are, and I don't mean in the middle of southwest Texas."

"There's worse places."

"If you say so, honey."

"Trust me on it."

"I do trust you, Sailor. Like I ain't never trusted nobody before. It's scary sometimes. You ain't got much maybe or might in you."

Sailor laughed, and put his arm over Lula, brushing her cheek with his hand.

"Maybe and might are my little brothers," he said. "I gotta set 'em a good example, is all."

"It ain't really them worries me, it's those cousins, never and ever, make me shake."

"We'll be all right, peanut, long as we got room to move."

Lula clucked her tongue twice.

"Know what?" she said.

"Uh?"

"I don't know that I completely enjoy you callin' me peanut so much."

Sailor laughed. "Why's that?"

"Puts me so far down on the food chain?"

Sailor looked at her.

"Really, Sail. I know how you mean it to be sweet, but I was thinkin' how everything can eat a peanut and a peanut don't eat nothin'. Makes me sound so tiny, is all."

"How you want, honey," he said.

WELCOME TO BIG TUNA

BIG TUNA, TEXAS, POP. 305, sits 125 miles west
of Biarritz, 125 miles east of Iraaq, and 100 miles north of
the Mexican border on the south fork of the Esperanza
trickle. Sailor cruised the Bonneville through the streets
of Big Tuna, eyeballing the place.

"This looks like a lucky spot, sweetheart," he said.
"Whattaya think?"

"Not bad," said Lula. "Long as you're not large on cool
breezes. Must be a hundred and ten and it ain't even noon
yet."

"Hundred twelve, to be exact. What it said on the
Iguana County Bank buildin' back there. And that's
prob'ly two degrees or more shy of the actual temp.
Chamber of commerce don't like to discourage visitors,
so they set it low."

"I can understand that, Sail. After all, there's a big
difference between a hundred twelve and a hundred fourteen."

Sailor circled back and stopped the car in front of the
Iguana Hotel, a two-story, whitewashed wooden building with the Texas state flag draped over the single porch
above the entrance.

"This'll do," he said.

The second-floor room Sailor and Lula rented was

simple: double bed, dresser, mirror, chair, sink, toilet, bathtub (no shower), electric fan, window overlooking the street.

"Not bad for eleven dollars a day," said Sailor.

"No radio or TV," said Lula. She stripped off the spread, tossed it in a corner and sat down on the bed. "And no AC."

"Fan works."

"Now what?"

"Let's go down to the drugstore and get a sandwich. Find out about where to look for work."

"Sailor?"

"Yeah?"

"This ain't exactly my most thrillin' notion of startin' a new life."

They ordered bologna and American cheese on white with Cokes at the counter of Bottomley's Drug.

"Pretty empty today," Sailor said to the waitress, whose plastic name tag had KATY printed on it.

"Ever'body's over to the funeral," Katy said. "This is kind of a sad day around here."

"We just got into town," said Lula. "What happened?"

"Buzz Dokes, who run a farm here for twenty years, died somethin' horrible. Only forty-four."

"How'd he go?" asked Sailor.

"Bumblebees got him. Buzz was on his tractor Monday mornin' when a swarm of bees lit on his head and knocked him off his seat. He fell underneath the mower and the blades chopped him up in four unequal parts. Run over a bee mound and they just rose up and attacked him. Poor Buzz. Tractor trampled him and kept goin', went through a fence and smacked into the side of a Messican's house. Took it clean off the foundation."

"That's about the most unpleasant incident I heard of lately," said Lula.

"There's always some strange thing or other happenin' in Big Tuna," Katy said. "I've lived here all my life, forty-one years, except for two years in Beaumont, and I could put together some book about this town. It wouldn't all be pretty, I tell you. But it's a sight better than bein' in a place like Beaumont, where people come down the street you don't know 'em and never will. I like bein' in a place where I know who I'm gonna see every day. What are you kids doin' here?"

"Lookin' for work," said Sailor.

"Any kind in particular?"

"I'm pretty fair with cars, trucks. Never done no ranchin', though, or farmin'."

"You might talk to Red Lynch. He's got a garage just two blocks up the street here, 'cross from the high school. Called Red's. He might have somethin', seein' as how the boys he usually hires don't last too long before they take off for Dallas or Houston. Not enough goin' on to keep 'em here. Red oughta be back from Buzz's funeral in a half hour or so."

"Thanks, Katy, I'll check it out. Tell me, why's this town named Big Tuna? There ain't no body of water around here woulda ever had no tuna in it."

Katy laughed. "That's for sure. All we got's wells and what falls from the sky, which ain't been a whole heck of a lot lately. The Esperanza's dry half the year. No, it's named after an oilman, Earl 'Big Tuna' Bink, who bought up most of Iguana County back in the twenties. Used to be called Esperanza Spring, only there ain't no spring, just like there ain't no tuna. Bink'd go off on fishin' trips to California, Hawaii and Australia and such, and have these big mounted fish shipped back here to his ranch. He died when I was ten. The whole county went to his funeral. Ever'body called him Big Tuna. There's a oil portrait of him hangin' in the Iguana County Bank, which he owned. Where you-all from?"

"Florida," said Sailor. "Orlando, Florida."

"Boy, my grandkids'd sure love to go to that Disney World. You been there plenty, I guess."

"Lots of times."

Lula sucked on the straw in her Coke and stared at Sailor. He turned and smiled at her, then went back to making conversation with Katy. Lula suddenly felt sick to her stomach.

"I'm gonna go back up to the room and lie down, Sailor," she said. "This heat makes me tired."

"Okay, honey, I'll see you later."

"Bye," Lula said to Katy.

"Have a nice *siesta,* dear," said Katy.

Outside everything looked cooked, like the white of a fried egg, with brown edges. Lula walked very slowly the half block to the Iguana Hotel and barely made it up the stairs into the room before she threw up.

THE BIG NOWHERE

"YOU RED?"

Sailor was talking to the sweaty, grimy back of a stocky, shirtless man whose shoulders, arms and head were buried under the hood of a brown 1983 Buick Regal.

"No," the man grunted, without extricating himself. "Inside."

Sailor stood in what looked to be a junkyard. Greasy or rusting automobile parts, bottles, cans, torn-up couches, seatless or one-legged chairs, discarded screws, nails, springs, empty cartons, crushed cardboard boxes and other assorted garbage were strewn on the ground in front of Red's Garage. A fat red dog of indeterminate breed with only one ear slept by the entrance. A tall, skinny man in his early thirties with wild, uncombed hair the color of a pomegranate, wearing a grease-smeared white-and-red Hook-'em-Horns tee shirt and dark grey work pants, walked out of the corrugated-metal Butler building.

"You lookin' for me?" he said.

"If you're Red."

"Well, I ain't Blackie," said Red, with a smile.

Sailor held out his right hand to shake.

"Name's Sailor Ripley. Katy over at the drugstore thought you might maybe have some work I could do."

Red extended his own oil-blackened right hand and shook.

"Business ain't like the weather," he said.

"Meanin'?"

"Ain't real hot right now. Rex there, though," said Red, nodding toward the half-naked man burrowed into the Buick, "is about to relocate to San Angelo. I might could use a man when he does."

"When'd that be?"

"Week, ten days. Hey, Rex, how long till you head for Angelo?"

Rex pulled his head out from beneath the hood. He wiped his face with a crusty black rag and spat tobacco juice on the ground next to the sleeping red dog. The dog didn't twitch. Rex had a blue, quarter-inch-width scar across his nose.

"Susie's ma says we can have the trailer middle of next week," he said.

"You good with engines?" Red asked Sailor.

"I ain't no Enzo Ferrari, but they used to call me Wrench when I was a kid. Raced C Stock."

"We'll see how she goes then when Rex takes off. Check back."

Two men, both about forty, walked up to Red. One of them wore a grey baseball cap with a Confederate flag on it and the other had on an LBJ straw Stetson.

"How's it look?" said the man in the Stetson.

"Reckon the head's cracked, like I thought."

"Shit, that's what I was afraid of. It'll take some time then."

Red nodded. "It will," he said.

The man wearing the Rebel cap knelt down next to the fat red dog and scratched behind the dog's remaining ear.

"How you doin', Elvis?" he said to the dog. "Don't look like Elvis ever missed a meal, Red."

"He's always been regular," said Red.

Elvis didn't move. A dozen flies rested on his face.

"Anybody need a beer?" asked Rex, taking a six-pack of Bud from a small Kelvinator set up on blocks just inside the garage. He handed one to each man, kept a can for himself, tore the plastic ring off and tossed it on the ground and put one beer back in the refrigerator.

"I'm Buddy," said the man with the cap to Sailor, "and this here's Sparky."

Sailor introduced himself to Sparky and Buddy and Rex. They all shook hands or nodded and moved out of the sun to drink their beers.

"You fellas live here?" Sailor asked Sparky and Buddy.

Buddy laughed. "Feels like it now, don't it, Spark?"

"Car broke down," said Sparky. "The Buick over there. We been here a week while Red and Rex been troubleshootin' it."

"Where you headed?"

"California," said Buddy. "We live in San Bruno, south of San Francisco. Sparky's a plumber and I drive a produce delivery truck."

"Shoot, how'd y'all end up down here?"

"Deep in the Big Nowhere, you mean?" said Sparky. "Long story." He took a swig from his can.

"Short version is that Spark's dad died in Tampa," said Buddy, "left him his car. Spark and I flew down for the funeral and afterward packed up the stuff Spark wanted to keep, loaded it into the Buick. Made it far as Seguin, just the other side of San Antonio, before the car started actin' up. Tuned it there and thought we was okay, but around Kerrville the damn thing overheated somethin' fierce. Clicked off the AC and pushed it too far, I guess. Twenty-four miles west of Big Tuna it stuttered and boiled up. I was drivin' and pulled off on a dirt access road. There was nothin' around but dust and snakes and it was about a hundred and twenty with no hope of shade."

Sparky laughed. "This pickup comes along and Buddy throws himself in front of it, wavin' his arms like a weighted-down vulture tryin' to take off."

"No shit," said Buddy. "We woulda died out there. So the guy in the pickup used his towrope to pull us back to the Big Tuna here, where we've placed our fate in the unhygienic but supposedly automotively capable hands of Inman 'Don't Call Me Inman' Red Lynch. How about yourself?"

"My girl and I are lookin' for a place to settle," said Sailor. "We're bunked down at the Iguana Hotel."

"So are we," said Sparky. "It's the only hotel in Big Tuna. Have you met Bobby 'Just Like the Country' Peru yet?"

"No, we just got in a hour and a half ago."

"You will," Buddy said. "He's the Mr. Fix-it at the Iguana. His truck broke down here a couple of months ago."

"Escaped con," said Rex. "Man got some serious prison tattoos."

"Ever'body got a past," said Red.

"Just some got more future in 'em than others," Buddy said.

"That ain't no lie," said Rex.

Sailor finished his beer, stood it on the ground and stepped on it, crushing it flat.

"Been nice meetin' y'all," he said. " 'Preciate the beer. I'll be seein' y'all soon."

"Very soon," said Buddy.

"One thing about bein' in Big Tuna," said Sparky, "you don't have much choice about who you see and who you don't."

Sailor found Lula asleep on the bed. There was a terrible odor in the room and a big damp spot on the rug near the door.

"That you, Sail, honey?"

"The only one."

Lula opened her eyes and looked at Sailor.

"You see Red?"

"Uh huh. Met him and a bunch of boys. What's that smell?"

"I barfed. Tried to clean it with Ivory and water but it didn't do much good."

"You sick?"

"A little, I think. Darlin'?"

"Yeah?"

"Come sit by me."

Sailor went over and sat on the bed.

"I don't know that this is the right place for us."

Sailor stroked Lula's head.

"It ain't gonna be forever, peanut."

Lula closed her eyes.

"I know, Sailor. Nothin' is."

ONE NIGHT IN NACOGDOCHES

"TOO LATE FOR THE RIOT, Johnnie boy, as usual."

Johnnie and Marietta were having dinner with Johnnie's friend Eddie Guidry in Joe R's Steak 'n' Shrimp in Nacogdoches, Texas.

"Kinda riot, Eddie?"

"Cops killed a black kid who'd stuck up a 7-Eleven, durin' the process of which he'd coldcocked a seventy-eight-year-old white woman with a pistol. She died. Kid got away but cops in Bossier City caught him, shipped him back to Nacogdoches, where some fool deputy beat him to death. Boy was fifteen. One of the local black attorneys, woman named Rosetta Coates, who's very powerful around here, graduated top of her class at Austin, made a speech about it got the whole town excited. Result was thirteen dead, eleven of 'em blacks. Stores burned, looted. Regular Mardi Gras, Texas-style."

"Johnnie tells me you're a writer, Mr. Guidry," said Marietta.

"Yes, ma'am."

"May I inquire as to what type of writin' you do?"

"Adventure novels, action stuff. Doubt you'd be much interested in 'em."

"Would I have heard of any?"

"Had a pretty near best-seller three, four years ago, called *Death Chopper*. Did damn good in convenience stores."

"That's interestin', Mr. Guidry. I wasn't aware books were sold in those places."

"Hell, yes. Ain't no bookstores left, practically. Buy you a toothbrush, quart of low-fat, double A batteries, pack of Trojan-enz, *TV Guide* and a paperback best-seller all in the same run."

"Eddie and I met in the service, Marietta," said Johnnie. "We were together at Fort Jackson, then again in Nam."

"Do you write much about your experiences in Vietnam, Mr. Guidry?"

"No, ma'am, not really. In order for 'em to sell they gotta be like comic books. I ain't what you'd classify as a *serious* writer, unless you're talkin' money only, and *that's* sure as shit serious! No, Johnnie's the literary one. You ever read any of his stories?"

"Why, Johnnie," said Marietta, "why ain't you ever showed your writin' to me?"

Johnnie just shook his head and cut into his steak.

"He's got the ideas, this old boy," said Eddie. "Wish I had 'em."

From her room at the Ramada Inn after dinner, Marietta called Dalceda Delahoussaye.

"Dal? How you, honey?"

"Marietta? Where are you?"

"Nacogdoches, Texas, of all places. Johnnie wanted to stop by and see a old friend of his named Eddie Guidry. You ever heard of him? Says he writes war novels."

"Louis read one of 'em. *Chopped to Death*, I think it was. Man's a multimillionaire, Marietta. He single?"

"Divorced with four children. Lives with a Mexican girl, Johnnie told me. Daughter of the fam'ly maid. Prob'ly all of fourteen years old."

Dal laughed. "Nothin' we can do about them young ones, Marietta. They just keep on comin'."

"Mr. Guidry ain't my type. Man's got hair, Dal, I swear! Hairline's down on the bridge of his nose and hair's stickin' out on him from ever'where, 'specially his ears. Pretty disgustin'."

"What about Lula?"

"Johnnie's got a guy in San Antonio checkin' around. We know they're runnin' low on money, so they'll have to stop someplace and work. Johnnie's ninety percent positive they're headed west. His associate in San Antone's makin' calls. Cover more ground with a telephone than you can in a car, Johnnie says."

"Sounds smart. You sleepin' with him, Marietta?"

"Oh, Dal, hush. We got separate rooms at the Ramada."

"Last night I come in the bedroom and Louis is sleepin', but he's got this big ol' hard-on. Well, big for Louis, anyway. So I climb over him real careful and take it out of his pajama bottoms and stick it in me."

"Dal!" Marietta squealed. "You're lyin'!"

"How else am I gonna get him to do it? Anyway, he woke up quick and come quicker, so it was nothin' to write home about. I tell you, Marietta, we oughta go down to Old Mexico and get us a couple maraca-playin' beach boys like Ava Gardner had in that movie? We ain't dead or dried up yet but it won't be long. I'm *serious,* Marietta."

"I'm tired, Dal. I'll let you know soon's I find out somethin'."

"Think about what I'm sayin' now, okay? Love you, Marietta. You take care."

"I will, Dal. Bye."

READER'S STORY

"You ever see that Errol Flynn movie, *Objective Burma?*" Sailor asked.

Lula was sitting in a chair, painting her toenails.

"Not that I recall," she said.

"Flynn and a group of soldiers is about to jump from an airplane into the jungle near Mandalay or somewhere during World War Two," said Sailor, "and one of the guys asks Flynn, 'What if my chute doesn't open?' And Flynn says, 'Well, you'll be the first on the ground.'"

Lula laughed. "He was awful handsome," she said, "even if he did have a mustache? I never have cared for facial hair on a guy unless he was so ugly it covered him up."

Sailor got up from the bed and began putting on his clothes.

"Let's go have some dinner, peanut," he said. "I'm ready."

"My toenails gotta dry first, Sailor. Tell me a story while we're waitin'."

"What kinda story, darlin'?"

"Anythin' you got to say interests me," said Lula. "You know that."

"You really are dangerously cute, honey," Sailor said. "I gotta admit it."

Lula giggled and stretched out on the bed, dangling her feet over the edge.

Sailor sat down in a chair by the window. He could see the heat waves roll down the street.

"Up at Pee Dee I met a guy named Reader O'Day," he said. "Reader was in for doin' in his common-law wife. Got seventeen to life for second-degree murder."

"What kinda name is Reader?" asked Lula.

"He's called that on account of he reads a lot. I never heard his Christian name that I can recall. He's always readin' some book that his people send him. Reader went to college. He's about forty-six now and he still reads books."

"That's amazin'," said Lula. "I mean, it's probably pretty rare for a criminal of any kind."

"For a long time he was readin' books by a dead French guy. Reader told me all this guy's books were parts of what was called *Rememberin' Things Past*. I think that's the name. Anyway, accordin' to Reader, the author got the idea for writin' down all this stuff just after he ate a cookie."

"A cookie?"

"Yeah. The French guy bit into a cookie and a whole flood of things he remembered filled up his brain and he wrote 'em down. Reader said the guy was sick a lot and he was still writin' when he died, right up to the last second."

Lula clucked her tongue a couple of times.

"Why'd Reader clock his old lady?" she asked.

Sailor shook his head and whistled softly through his teeth.

"That's a whole story," he said. "Seems they had a daughter that didn't get along too good with the mother, and Reader stuck it out for the kid's sake. According to him, the woman acted pretty violent toward the little girl and toward Reader, too. Reader said once she attacked him with a hot iron and another time with a chain saw."

"Sounds like that movie I wouldn't go see," said Lula.

"Reader figured he ought to stay around to protect his daughter. For a while they lived down around Morgan City and he worked in the oil fields. When the oil business went belly-up he moved back to the Piedmont and worked the tobacco. The woman worked once in a while as a helper in a hospital. Reader said she was just Alabama trash and he'd picked up with her in the first place at a time when he wasn't feelin' none too high on himself neither. After the daughter was born, though, he kinda changed his ways."

"He must come from good people?" said Lula. "After all, he did go to college."

"I believe he said his daddy was a doctor," Sailor said. "So prob'ly he was a disappointment to his folks, out kickin' around the oil fields and doin' jobs anybody could be doin'. Anyhow, the woman kept buggin' him to marry her and make their daughter legitimate. Reader didn't want to get hitched to this woman and told her he was only still with her 'cause of the kid. This went on for some time, I guess, her after him to marry her and him refusin'. One day when the daughter, who was about ten years old at the time, was at school or somewhere, Reader's old lady come at him with a rifle and threatened to kill him unless he married her. When he told her to back off, she fired the gun and just missed him. He said the bullet grazed his left ear and smacked into the wall behind him. He grabbed the rifle away from her and went a little crazy."

"You mean he shot her?" said Lula.

"Five or six times," said Sailor. "Guess he got so mad he just stood over her and kept cockin' the rifle and firin' till it was empty. Then he made a real mistake."

"As if pluggin' half a dozen slugs into the lady wasn't enough," Lula said.

"Instead of callin' the cops," said Sailor, "and pleadin' self-defense or justifiable homicide and bein' driven out of his mind, he wrapped up her body in a shower curtain and buried it underneath the house."

"What'd he tell his daughter?"

"Just that her mother'd gone away for a vacation or somethin'. Reader dropped her with his folks and took off. Went to New York, Chicago, Las Vegas, all over. He got caught when he tried to sneak back and see his daughter."

"How'd the police find the body?"

"That's the good part," Sailor said. "They didn't. At least not until Reader told 'em where he'd stashed it. They went ahead and prosecuted him based on circumstantial evidence. In the middle of the trial, with Reader thinkin' he was gonna walk, they subpoenaed his mama, and when she refused to testify they popped her in the slam. She's a older woman in poor health, so she can't take more'n a week. When she gets out she admits that Reader told her about the shootin'. Reader testifies that his common-law wife attacked him first and that she got shot by accident while they was strugglin' for the weapon. He tells 'em where the body's buried, they dig it up, and find her full of holes fired point-blank. Put together with his havin' hit the road, this don't do Reader no good. The jury just wasn't about to buy his side of the matter. He told me most of the jurors was women, and when he said in court that his common-law wife used to get riled up regular whenever she got on the rag, they looked about set to lynch him right now. Reader was prob'ly the nicest fella I met at Pee Dee. Your toes dry yet, peanut?"

NIGHT AND DAY AT THE IGUANA HOTEL

"HOW DO YOU GET SIXTEEN HAITIANS into a Dixie cup?" said Sparky.

"How?" asked Lula.

"Tell 'em it floats."

Sailor, Lula, Sparky and Buddy were sitting in the lobby of the Iguana Hotel at ten P.M., sharing Sparky's fifth of Ezra Brooks and shooting the shit.

"Sparky's big on Florida jokes," said Buddy.

"You need a active sense of humor to survive in the Big Tuna," said Sparky.

Bobby Peru walked in and came over.

"Hey, everybody," he said.

"Sailor, Lula, this here's the man himself," said Buddy. "Bobby, this is Sailor and Lula, the most recent strandees, economic variety."

Bobby nodded to Lula and offered a hand to Sailor.

"Bobby Peru, just like the country."

Sparky and Buddy laughed.

"Accordin' to Red and Rex," said Buddy, "Bobby's the most excitin' item to hit Big Tuna since the '86 cyclone sheared the roof off the high school."

"Only in town two months and there ain't a young

123

thing around don't know how that cobra tattoo works, right, Bob?" Sparky said.

Bobby laughed. He had a lopsided grin that exposed only three brownish front teeth on the upper right side of his mouth. He had dark, wavy hair and a small, thin nose that bent slightly left. His eyebrows were long and tapered and looked as if they'd been drawn on. What frightened Lula about Bobby Peru were his eyes: flat black, they reflected no light. They were like heavy shades, she thought, that prevented people from seeing inside. Lula guessed that he was about the same age as Sparky and Buddy, but Bobby was the kind of person who would look the same when he was forty-five as he did when he was twenty.

"You from Texas, Mr. Peru?" Lula asked.

Bobby pulled up a chair and poured himself a shot glass full of whisky.

"I'm from all over," he said. "Born in Tulsa, raised in Arkansas, Illinois, Indiana, lived in Oregon, South Dakota, Virginia. Got people in Pasadena, California, who I was headin' to see when my Dodge busted a rod. Still meanin' to get out there."

"You was in the marines, huh?" said Sailor, noticing a USMC tattoo on Bobby's right hand.

Bobby looked down at his hand, flexed it.

"Four years," he said.

"Bobby was at Cao Ben," said Sparky.

"What's Cao Ben?" asked Lula.

"How old are you?" Buddy asked her.

"Twenty."

"Bunch of civilians got killed," said Bobby. "March 1968. We torched a village and the government made a big deal out of it. Politicians tryin' to get attention. Put the commandin' officer on trial for murder. Only problem was, there weren't no such persons as civilians in that war."

"Lotta women and kids and old people died at Cao Ben," said Buddy.

Bobby sipped the whisky and closed his eyes for several seconds before reopening them and looking at Buddy.

"You was on a ship, pardner. Hard to make contact with the people when you're off floatin' in the Gulf of Tonkin. It weren't simple."

"Saw Perdita this afternoon," said Sparky. "Came by Red's lookin' for you."

"Had some business over by Iraaq," said Bobby. "I'm just about to go check on her now."

He stood up and set the shot glass on his chair.

"Good meetin' you," Bobby said to Sailor and Lula. "*Adiós,* boys."

He walked out.

After Bobby was gone, Lula said, "Somethin' in that man scares me."

"Bobby's got a way," said Buddy.

"Can't shake that institution odor," Sparky said, and poured himself another shot.

Lula put a hand on Sailor's leg.

"Darlin', I still ain't feelin' so well," she said. "I'm goin' to bed."

"I'll come along," said Sailor.

They said good night to Sparky and Buddy and went upstairs.

In the room, Sailor said, "Man, that barf smell don't fade fast."

"I'll get some white vinegar to rub on it tomorrow, honey, take care of it."

Lula went into the bathroom and stayed there for a long

time. When she came out, Sailor asked if there was anything he could do for her.

"No, I don't think so, Sail. I just need to lie down."

Lula listened to Sailor brush his teeth, then urinate into
the toilet and flush it.

"Sailor?" she said as he climbed into bed. "You know
what?"

"I know you ain't particularly pleased bein' here."

"Not that. Might be I'm pregnant."

Sailor rolled over and looked into Lula's eyes.

"It's okay by me, peanut."

"Well, nothin' personal, but I ain't so sure it's okay
by me."

Sailor lay down on his back.

"Really, Sailor, it ain't nothin' against you. I love you."

"Love you, too."

"I know. Just I'm sorta uncomfortable about the way
some things is goin', and this don't help soothe me."

Sailor got out of bed and went over by the window. He
sat down in the chair and looked out. Bobby Peru and a
Mexican woman with black hair longer than Lula's were
parked across the street in a maroon 1971 Eldorado convertible with the top down. Sailor watched as the woman
pulled a knife out of her purse and tried to stick Bobby
with it. He took the knife away from her and tossed it.
She got out of the car and ran. Bobby fired up the Eldo
and drove after her.

"I know this ain't easy, Lula," Sailor said, "but I ain't
gonna let things get no worse, I promise."

THE EARLY
YEARS

"I'VE ALWAYS BEEN FASCINATED by the ways people do business, Marietta. When they discuss large sums of money they lower their voices, they whisper. It don't matter whether the sonofabitch'll be dead or too old to spend the money he might make eventually from a deal, it's the *thought* of it that counts. The reverence, the absolute reverence some people have for money amazes me. For the mere mention of large sums, as if the money would disappear if they referred to it in less than the most respectful terms. I tell ya, Marietta, the only two things anybody seems to be interested in anymore are money and losin' weight."

Johnnie and Marietta were drinking coffee in a booth in the Bad Bull truckstop diner in Biarritz.

"Johnnie, all I care about right now is Lula."

A waitress came over and refilled Johnnie's cup. Marietta covered hers with her right hand.

"I'm fine, honey," she said to the waitress, who was about seventeen years old. "Don't she remind you of Lula?" Marietta asked Johnnie. "She got the same buttery skin."

The waitress smiled and put their check on the table and walked away.

"Listen, Marietta, there really ain't no point in your hangin' out on the road like this. I 'preciate the fact you enjoy my company and all, but until I got some more concrete information to go on, you're just wastin' your time."

"I'd go crazy sittin' home. Least this way I'm *doin'* somethin'."

Johnnie sighed and sipped his coffee.

"Truth is," he said, "I'm gonna give this squirrel hunt about another couple days, is all. Week, maybe. I got work waitin' on me in Charlotte. Maceo in San Antonio can keep after it and I'll be callin' people around the country might be able to help out. You can bet Sailor's parole officer's reported him missin', too."

Marietta's eyes filled with tears and her nose began to run.

"Marietta, you're drippin' in your coffee."

Johnnie handed her a napkin. Marietta took it and wiped her eyes and blew her nose.

"I hate feelin' helpless, Johnnie. I hate it worse'n anything. Dal was against my comin', too."

"We'll hang in a touch longer, like I said. Maybe we'll run onto a lead right quick."

"I got to use the ladies' room."

Johnnie took his notebook out of his pocket and looked over what he'd written the night before in the motel. He'd decided to write about his childhood, beginning with his earliest sexual memories.

MY EARLY YEARS

by Johnnie Farragut

When I was very young, three or four years old, I would imagine that I was a leopard, a panther, crawling around on the floor, from which vantage point I would attempt to look under women's dresses. Once our maid caught me doing this to her. She wore stockings and I could see up to where they were fastened onto her garter belt and the large black area between her legs. She squeezed my head between her knees and laughed.

"Sniff it, baby," she said. "Sniff it good. You won't ever get enough."

I panicked, I was frightened and tried to pull my head loose, but it was stuck. She had me firmly between her thighs. The only direction I could move was up, so I pushed higher under her dress until my face was against the soft wet cotton of her panties. She started to move so that my nose rubbed against her clitoris, making her pants wetter, then harder over my mouth and chin. I was choking, I could barely breathe, but the iron grip of her legs held me helpless.

All I could see was black and my face was sticky. The smell was overpowering, like in a stable. At first I thought it was like that, like piles of horse manure, but then I knew it was different, like nothing I'd smelled before. I thought I was dying, I was suffocating, and she spread her legs slightly and held my head into her as she breathed faster and made more horrible sounds, rubbing herself back and forth over my hair. Finally she released me. I didn't die, I fell back on the floor and opened my eyes. I looked up at her and she was grinning.

"Come on, baby," she said, holding a hand down to me. "We better go wash your face."

Marietta came back and sat down.

"When you gonna let me read your writin', Johnnie?"

Johnnie closed his notebook and put it back in his coat.

"One day soon, maybe. When I got somethin' I think'll interest you."

"Prob'ly more things interest me than you think."

"I ain't never sold you short, Marietta, you know that."

Marietta smiled. "I know, Johnnie," she said. "I most certainly do."

MOSQUITOES

SAILOR WAS CHANGING THE OIL in the Bonneville when Bobby Peru pulled up in the maroon Eldo.

"Need a hand?"

"Thanks, Bobby, about done."

Sailor slid the pan of dirty oil out from underneath the
Bonneville.

"Where's the best place to dump this?"

"Around back. Come on, I'll show ya."

Sailor picked up the pan and followed Bobby down the
side of the Iguana Hotel.

"Empty it right in them weeds. Ain't nobody comes
back here anyway. You about ready for a beer?"

"Sure, Bobby, that'd be fine."

"Let's go by Rosarita's. You been there yet?"

"No, haven't heard of it."

"Thought maybe Sparky and Buddy'd taken ya. Come
on, I'll drive."

They got into the Cadillac and Bobby guided it slowly
along Travis Street, Big Tuna's main drag.

"This your car?" Sailor asked.

Bobby laughed. "Hell no, belongs to Tony Durango. I
been datin' his sister, Perdita, lately. Tony's up in Fort
Worth with his wife's family for a couple weeks, so he's
lettin' me use it. Where's that pretty little lady of yours
today?"

"Restin' in our room. She ain't been feelin' well."

"Sorry to hear it. Women are always havin' some kinda physical problem. Been my experience with 'em."

Bobby turned off Travis onto Ruidoso Road and gunned the Eldo up to seventy. He rodded it for five minutes until they came to a closed-down filling station, where Bobby slowed down and circled around behind the building. A half dozen pickup trucks and three or four cars were parked in a row and Bobby wedged the Cad in between a tan Ford Ranger and a white Ranchero.

"Used to be this was a Mobil," said Bobby as they got out of the car. "Man converted it into a private club and named it after his wife. She left him and he shot himself. The wife owns it now."

They entered a long, dark room where a dozen men, most of them wearing cowboy hats, sat on stools at a bar drinking beer out of frosted mugs.

"No hard liquor here," Bobby told Sailor. "Just beer."

They claimed two stools and Bobby said, "Coupla Stars, Jimmy."

The bartender, who was no taller than five feet five or six and weighed at least two hundred and forty pounds, brought over two bottles and two mugs.

"How ya be, Bobby?" he said. "Who's your *amigo*?"

"Sailor, meet Jimmy, otherwise known as Mr. Four-by-Four. He's always lookin' out for the patrons' welfare. Won't let ya drink no more'n forty, fifty beers, 'less you ain't drivin'."

"Howdy, Sailor," said Jimmy. "Enjoy yourself."

He walked back toward the other end of the bar.

"Thought you said this was a private club," Sailor said to Bobby. "How come I'm allowed in without bein' a member?"

"You black?"

"No."

"You an Indian?"

"No."

"Then you're a member."

"I've Got a Tiger by the Tail" by Buck Owens was playing on the jukebox, and Bobby kept time rapping his knuckles on the bar.

"Three or four millionaires in here right now," he said.

Sailor looked around at the other customers. All of them were modestly dressed.

"They look like a bunch of good ol' boys to me," said Sailor. "I guess it's oil money, huh?"

"Oil, gas, cattle, farmin'. Ain't nobody shows off around here. Iguana County's one of the richest in Texas."

"Wouldn't'a guessed it, that's sure."

"Ready for another?"

"Why not?"

When they were on their fifth round, Bobby went over to the jukebox and dropped in some quarters.

"Q-seven," he said, climbing back onto his stool, "three times. Pee Wee King's 'Waltz of Regret,' my favorite tune."

Pee Wee's steel guitar rippled through the cigarette haze and buzzed around Sailor's head. His reflection wobbled in the long mirror behind the bar.

"I been studyin' a situation over in Iraaq," said Bobby. "Take two men to handle it."

"What's that?"

"Feed store keeps up to five K in their safe. Need me a good boy for backup. Even split. You interested?"

Sailor knew he was slightly drunk. He rotated his head on his shoulders and flexed his back muscles. He stared at Bobby and worked hard to focus his eyes.

"Be easy, Sailor. There's two employees. I take one in

the back to open the safe, you keep the other'n covered. You ain't plannin' on raisin' a fam'ly in Big Tuna, are ya?"

"Lula tell you she's pregnant?"

Bobby grinned, showing those three brown teeth.

"Couple grand or more'd give you two a leg up. Get you to the West Coast, Mexico, most anyplace, with a few dollars in your jeans. I got it figured good, Sailor. Simple's best."

"I ain't sure, Bobby. I got to consider this careful."

"I respect you for it, Sailor. Don't do a man no good to go in on a deal with less'n a full tank. You had enough?"

Sailor finished his beer and nodded. "Have now."

"Come on outside, I got somethin' to show ya."

Bobby looked around before he opened the trunk of the Eldorado. He peeled back a brown army blanket and said, "That's a double-barreled, sawed-off Ithaca shotgun with a carved pistol grip stock wrapped with adhesive tape. Next to it's a cold Smith and Wesson thirty-two handgun with a six-inch barrel. These'll do 'er."

Bobby covered the weapons with the blanket and closed the trunk. He and Sailor got into the car. The sky was dark pink. Bobby turned on the radio as they drove, fiddling with the dial until it landed on a classical music station out of San Antonio playing Gottschalk's *Night in the Tropics.*

"I sometimes listen to this serious stuff," said Bobby. "Kills off the mosquitoes in my brain."

THE BLACK
ANGEL

SAILOR BENT OVER THE BED and kissed Lula's
hair above her left ear.

"Hi, hon," she said. "You been drinkin', huh?"

"Few beers is all. Feelin' any better?"

Lula rolled onto her back, stretched her arms in the air
and yawned.

"Can't tell yet. Where'd you go?"

"Smell's mostly gone. That vinegar really done the
job."

"Buddy and Sparky come by earlier."

"How they doin'?"

"Okay, I guess. Sparky said Red's promised to have
'em out of here by the weekend."

"Oughta make 'em happy."

"So where'd you say you was?"

"Went with Bobby."

Sailor went into the bathroom and washed his face.
Lula came in and sat on the toilet to pee.

"Hope you don't mind, Sail, I couldn't wait. What's
Mr. Peru Like the Country up to?"

"Not much."

"Don't think he ever been up to much good his whole
life."

Sailor laughed. "Maybe not."

"Sail?"

"Uh huh?"

"Let's leave here."

"We're goin' to, Lula, real soon."

"I mean tomorrow."

"We got about forty bucks, sweetheart. That'd get us to El Paso."

"Rather be in El Paso than Big Tuna."

Sailor walked out of the bathroom, took off his clothes and got into bed. Lula flushed the toilet, rinsed her face and hands, then came out and picked up her pack of cigarettes from the dresser.

"You shouldn't be smokin' if you're pregnant," said Sailor. "Ain't smart."

Lula stuck a More between her lips and lit it. She took a deep drag, blew out the smoke and stared at Sailor.

"Who says I'm smart?" she said. "You up to somethin' with Bobby Peru, Sailor?"

"What could I be up to, Lula?"

"He's a stone fuckin' criminal, honey, and you ain't."

Sailor laughed. "I killed Bob Ray Lemon, didn't I?"

"That was a accident. I bet both our asses Bobby Peru done murdered all kinds of people, and meant it, too."

"That was in Vietnam."

"He's the kind liked it."

"Lula, I got to get some sleep."

"Buddy told me about that thing at Cao Ben?"

"What?"

"Was a massacre. Soldiers there murdered old folks, women and babies, and dumped 'em in a trench. Bobby Peru prob'ly killed the most."

"Lula, he mighta did, I don't know. But it don't matter now. Lotta guys go outa control in a war and it ain't their fault."

Lula puffed hard on her cigarette.

"I sure enjoy smokin', Sailor. I hate that it's bad for you."

Sailor turned on his side, away from Lula, and pulled a pillow over his head.

"That Mexican woman, Perdita Durango, who's been goin' around with Bobby Peru? Did you know she drowned her own baby? Katy at the drugstore told me when I was out gettin' the vinegar."

"Anything else people told you today you ain't mentioned yet?"

"That man's a black angel, Sailor. You hook up with him, you'll regret it. If you live to."

"Thanks, darlin', I know you got my best interest in mind, and I 'preciate it sincerely. I love you, but I gotta sleep now."

Lula lit a second More off the first and stubbed out the butt on the dresser top.

"Shit," she said, softly. "Shit, shit, shit."

THE MEANING
OF LIFE

"OKAY, SPARK, HERE IT IS," Buddy said, putting his pen down on the counter. "My all-time top ten, in no particular order. 'Lucille' by Little Richard, 'Lonely Nights' by The Hearts, 'He's So Fine' by The Chiffons, 'Be My Baby' by The Ronettes, 'Sea of Love' by Phil Phillips, 'High Blood Pressure' by Huey 'Piano' Smith and The Clowns, 'It's Rainin'' by Irma Thomas, 'You're No Good' by Betty Everett, 'I'd Rather Go Blind' by Etta James, and 'Sittin' on the Dock of the Bay' by Otis Redding. What do you think?"

"I've always been partial to 'Sea of Love' myself," said Sparky. "But where's 'My Pretty Quadroon' by Jerry Lee Lewis? Just kiddin'. But how about 'Breathless,' at least? Where's Sam Cooke? Elvis? Chuck Berry? 'Just One Look' by Doris Troy? 'Stay' by Maurice Williams? 'I'm a King Bee' by Slim Harpo? Or 'Little Darlin'' by The Gladiolas? 'If You Lose Me, You'll Lose a Good Thing' by Barbara Lynn? Marvin Gaye? Little Miss Cornshucks? Sugar Pie DeSanto? The Beatles? The Stones?"

"Can't all be in the top ten. Those are the ones I'd take. Not meant to please anyone but myself. Besides, makin' lists helps pass the time."

Buddy and Sparky were sitting in Bottomley's Drug, drinking 7-Ups. The temperature outside was 115 degrees.

"Well, will you look at this," said Katy, who was standing behind the counter reading yesterday's *San Antonio Light*. "Knew someday somethin' like it would happen to him."

"Who you talkin' about?" Buddy asked.

"Joe Don Looney, the football player. Greatest halfback in Texas high school history. Here, take a look."

She handed the newspaper to Buddy.

" 'Joe Don Looney Dies In Crash,' " Buddy read aloud. " 'Joe Don Looney, a former college and pro football player known as a rebel both on and off the gridiron, died Saturday in a motorcycle accident in southwest Texas, officials said. Looney, forty-five, was killed when he failed to make a curve on State Highway 118, according to the Department of Public Safety. Looney was thrown clear of the motorcycle and hit a wire fence, reports said.' "

"Just like Lawrence of Arabia," said Sparky.

"Ain't never heard of no Arabia, Texas," said Katy.

" 'The accident occurred around eight-thirty A.M. about nine miles north of the town of Study Butte in rural Brewster County. He was pronounced dead at the scene. Looney attended Texas Christian briefly before enrolling and starring for Cameron Junior College in Oklahoma.' "

"Boy's life was never the same after he left Texas," Katy said.

" 'He made the All-Junior College All-Star team and was recruited by then–Oklahoma coach Bud Wilkinson. In 1962, Looney rushed for 852 yards and was named to the All-Big Eight Conference team, but Wilkinson asked him to leave the Sooners because of discipline problems. Looney appealed to Wilkinson and was allowed to stay.

But Looney was thrown off the team the next year when he decked an O.U. coach.' "

"He was one wild-ass kid, all right," said Katy.

" 'In the 1963 NFL draft, Looney was selected in the first round by the New York Giants. He played for three more pro teams, Baltimore, Detroit and Washington, before retiring.' "

Buddy folded the paper and put it down on the counter.

"Joe Don was a legend when I was a girl," said Katy. "Handsome, too. But he went off the deep end somewheres."

"He went to India," Buddy said, "and studied with a guru and became a vegetarian. I remember seein' a TV program not too long ago, like *The NFL Today,* that did a short feature on Looney. He'd taken a lot of drugs in the sixties, like most of us, and in the seventies went to India, found a teacher and changed his lifestyle. After a few years, he came back to Texas and built a ten-sided house in the desert. Each wall inside had a picture of his guru on it. He lived alone and spent most of his day prayin'. He prepared his own special food, was celibate and didn't take drugs or medicines of any kind. He told the TV reporter that everything he'd been taught as a kid, to be a tough, football-playin' chicken fried steak eater, was wrong. That's why he'd always had such a hard time, he said, because he'd never really believed it was what he was meant to be doin'."

"He was right," said Sparky. "At least he got to find out before he died of a heart attack from eatin' all that meat and pumpin' his body full of steroids."

"That boy was marked for an early death," said Katy, "however it happened. Findin' out the meanin' of life and all is fine, far as it goes, but dead's dead, you know what I mean?"

FRIENDS

"NICE OF YOU TO DROP BY," said Perdita.

Bobby let the screen door bang shut behind him as he came in.

"Told you I would."

Perdita sat down on the couch, shook a Marlboro from the pack on the coffee table and lit it with a red Bic. Bobby roamed around the living room. The taps on the heels and toes of his boots clacked loudly against the hardwood floor.

"You still riled?" asked Bobby.

Perdita laughed. "You still screwin' sixteen-year-olds in the ass?"

Bobby smiled and kept circling.

"Ain't never had no teenaged girl pull a blade on me."

"Wish I'd cut you up good."

"Heard from Tony?"

"Juana called. They're stayin' another week."

Bobby stopped walking and stared at a family photograph on the wall.

"Stayin' a few extra days in the cow town, huh? This you?"

Perdita turned her head and looked, then turned back.

"Yes."

"How old were you? Twelve?"

"Almost. Eleven and a half. Ten years ago in Corpus."

"Mm, mm. What a tasty thing you musta been."

"Nobody was tastin'."

"Shame."

Bobby turned around and leaned down and put his face next to Perdita's from behind.

"The cobra's waitin' to strike, *chica*," he said.

Perdita crossed her legs and smoked. Bobby lowered his hands into the front of her blouse and cupped her small breasts. Perdita pretended not to care. He rubbed her nipples with the tips of his fingers, making them become rigid. She burned the back of his left wrist with her cigarette.

Bobby jumped back, then grabbed Perdita's hair and pulled her over the couch onto the floor. Neither of them spoke. She tried to stand up but Bobby kept his right foot on her chest while he blew on the back of his wounded wrist. Perdita shoved his leg to one side and rolled away. She stood up and spit at him.

Bobby grinned. "I knew we could be friends again," he said.

ONE STEP BEYOND

LULA READ A MAGAZINE ARTICLE about Evel Knievel, the man who'd tried to jump a rocket-shaped motorcycle across the mile-wide, 600-foot-deep Snake River Canyon; over 150-foot-tall fountains in front of a Las Vegas hotel-casino; a baker's dozen double-decker buses in London, England; a shark-filled pool in the Chicago stockyards; and made several other remarkable attempts at vehicular glory. At the Snake River, Knievel had crashed against the side of a mountain. In all, he'd broken at least forty bones, including both arms and his pelvis, and endured numerous brain concussions. Knievel had more than a dozen steel plates in his body, the article said, and now walked with the use of a gold-knobbed sword-cane since an operation had left one of his legs a half-inch shorter than the other.

Patsy Cline got killed in some kind of wreck when she was real young, Lula remembered. Patsy used that slow curve in her voice to talk about one kind of crazy. This daredevil idea, though, went way beyond natural.

BOBBY'S
BAD DAY

"TAKE ONE OF THESE," Bobby Peru said, handing
a plastic-wrapped package to Sailor.

"What is it?"

"Panty hose. Work better'n stockin's. Pull one of the
legs down over your face and let the other leg trail behind
your head."

They were in the Eldorado, about two blocks away
from the Ramos Feed Store in Iraaq. Perdita was at the
wheel, Bobby was next to her and Sailor rode in back.
The top was up.

"Here's the pistol," said Bobby, taking the Smith and
Wesson out of his belt and passing it to Sailor. "Remember, soon as we get inside you keep that bad boy up where
those hicks can see it. Once they notice the Ithaca and the
Smith, they'll know we ain't foolin' with 'em."

Perdita tossed her cigarette out the window and imme-
diately took out another and lit it with the dashboard
lighter.

"Comin' up on it now, Bobby," she said.

Bobby slipped the panty hose over his head and ad-
justed it. His face looked crooked, distorted and flat, the
lips pancaked across the lower half and his hair plastered
down over his forehead like broken teeth on a comb.

"Come on!" Bobby stage-whispered, his head snapping toward Sailor like a striking asp's. "Get that mask on!"

Sailor ripped open the package and pulled a nylon leg over his head, stretching the calf part to fit.

Perdita pulled up in front of the store. The street was deserted.

"Keep it revved, Chiquita. We won't be long," Bobby said.

It was two o'clock in the afternoon and the sun took up the entire sky. As Sailor got out of the car, he felt the intense heat of the day for the first time. Until that moment, he'd been numb. Sailor had passed the preceding hours in a kind of trance, unaware of the temperature or anything other than the time. Fourteen hours, Bobby had said, that's when they'd go in. They'd be out at fourteen-oh-three and thirty seconds, he promised, with something in the neighborhood of five thousand dollars.

Bobby went in first, carrying a black canvas Sundog shoulder bag in his left hand. He raised the sawed-off shotgun with his right and in a firm voice said to the two men behind the counter, "Move into the back room, both of you. Now!"

They moved. Both in their mid-fifties, portly, with wire-rim glasses and crown-bald heads, the men looked like brothers.

"Stay here," Bobby told Sailor as he followed them. "Keep an eye on the door. If anyone comes in, herd 'em on back, quick."

Sailor held the Smith up high, where Bobby could see it if he looked. Behind him, Sailor could hear Bobby instructing one of the men to open the safe. Neither of the men, so far as Sailor could tell, had said a word.

An Iguana County deputy sheriff cruised up in a patrol car and parked it on an angle in front of the idling Eldo.

The deputy got out of his car and walked over to the driver's side of the Cadillac. He looked at Perdita through his aviator-style reflector Ray-Bans, smiled, and placed both of his hands on the rag top.

"Waitin' for somebody, miss?" he said.

"*Mi esposo,*" said Perdita. "He's in the feed store picking up some supplies."

"You'd best be careful of that cigarette, ma'am. It's about to burn down between your fingers."

Perdita stubbed out her Marlboro in the ashtray.

"*Gracias,* officer."

Bobby came out of the store in a hurry, still wearing the panty hose on his head, carrying the shoulder bag and the shotgun. Perdita jammed the gearshift into reverse and peeled out, knocking the deputy down. She floored the Eldo for fifty yards, braked hard, yanked it into drive and spun a mean yo-yo, fishtailing viciously but managing to keep the car under control. Perdita hit the accelerator again as hard as she could and never looked back.

The deputy came up on one knee with his revolver clasped in both hands. He fired his first shot into Bobby's right thigh and his second into Bobby's left hip. The shock of the initial slug caused Bobby to drop the bag. The impact of the second forced Bobby's right hand to twist sideways so that both barrels of the shotgun wedged under his chin. The Ithaca went off, blowing Bobby backwards through the RAMOS on the plate-glass window of the feed store.

Sailor had been right behind Bobby until he saw Perdita hightail it. As soon as he spotted the deputy, Sailor hit the ground, losing the Smith as he fell. He put his hands over his hosieried head and kept his face in the dirt until the deputy ordered him to stand up.

MARIETTA'S TREASURE

"Hello, Mace, it's Johnnie."

"Glad you called, boy. You still east of El Paso?"

"We're at the Best Western in Fort Stockton."

"Oughta take you about two hours to get to Lula. Just heard on the news that Sailor Ripley and another guy tried to stick up a feed store in Iraaq. They're holdin' Ripley in the Iguana County jail in Big Tuna. Deputy sheriff shot and killed the other one."

" 'Preciate it, Maceo. Be talkin' to ya."

"Anytime."

Lula was sitting on a bench in the waiting room of the Iguana County Courthouse when Johnnie and Marietta walked in. As soon as she saw Lula, Marietta ran over, sat down next to her and hugged and kissed her.

"Oh, baby, I was beginnin' to think I was never gonna see you again."

Tears were pouring down Marietta's cheeks. She held Lula to her and Lula did not resist.

"Sweetheart, I'm so sorry about all this. I know you think I'm a crazy old woman, but I was so worried!"

"You ain't old, Mama. Hello, Johnnie."

"Hello, Lula. How you holdin'?"

"I'm tired, just real, honest-to-Jesus dog-tired."

"You're comin' home, precious," said Marietta. "Johnnie's gonna drive us to the San Antonio airport."

"Mama, Sailor's in deep trouble here. I can't just leave him."

Marietta took Lula by the shoulders and looked straight at her. Lula's eyes were bloodshot, her hair was greasy and stringy, and her cheeks were pale.

"Oh, yes, you can," Marietta said.

LETTER FROM LULA

Sailor Ripley
#461208
Walls Unit
Huntsville, Texas 77340

Dearest Sailor Darling,

The first thing youll want to know is Im keeping the baby. Mama wasnt for it in the beginning but I think shes looking forward to it. Im gonna name it Pace no matter if its a boy or a girl. Pace Ripley sounds good dont it? Its kind of hard to believe that Pace will be ten years old when you get out.

What else can I tell you? Im feeling fine its not so terrible being with mama cause shes calmed down a lot. I think our running off that way scared her plenty and she has more respect for me now. She doesnt even speak poorly of you no more at least not so often. I explained to her how you was worried about us not having money and the idea of a baby and all and how of course it was no excuse for committing an armed robbery but there it is.

I hope its not too horrible for you inside the walls again I know how much you hate being confined. Is it

149

different in a Texas prison than it was at Pee Dee? I bet
it aint as pretty. The doctor here says I got to stay at
home while Im pregnant. Theres something wrong
with the way Im carrying the baby but if I keep still and
dont smoke and eat right which mama and her friend
Dalceda Delahoussaye are seeing to he says I should be
just fine. It sure is hard not to smoke. I miss my
Mores!!! I feel like Im kind of in prison too but I know
in six months itll be over and Ill have a son or daughter
to show for it. <u>Our</u> child!!

I hope you know it hurts me to not be able to visit
you all I can do is write letters which is OK I like
writing. Did you know that Johnnie Farragut is a
writer? Mama told me he showed her some stories and
things he wrote and that she liked them. She says he has
an interesting imagination.

Did Perdita Durango ever get caught? Ill bet shes in
Mexico now or somewhere out of the authorities reach.
I have to confess it dont bother me one little bit about
Bobby Peru being shot dead. He was one of them types
you could feel it was coming and he killed his share as
we know. Remember once I called him a black angel
well hes not in heaven Ill guarantee. If he is then I never
want to go <u>there</u>!!!

It was excellent of you to give yourself up the way you
did and not try to shoot it out youd be dead too and
never have got to see your child Pace. I hope this name is
all right with you Sailor if its not tell me and Ill think it
over some more but I love it and certainly hope you do.

Im going to take a nap now. Your probably thinking
about how I was always sleeping at the end there in the
Iguana Hotel and now I still am but the doctor says
sometimes being pregnant makes the mother be that
way and Im one of them. I love you Sailor. I dont know
how much or what it means though I miss you an awful

bunch sometimes I know your thinking about me cause I can feel it. I miss your not being around to call me peanut nobody else ever called me that.

Like I said I have to rest again. Its not really so simple to write like this at least not like it was before when you was at Pee Dee cause that was for only two years not ten. Time dont really fly honey does it?

Love,
your Lula

LETTER
FROM SAILOR

Lula P. Fortune
127 Reeves Avenue
Bay St. Clement, N.C. 28352

Dear Lula,

It is fine with me about the baby as you already know. And Pace being your family name and all is just right. What about a middle name if it is a boy after my grandaddy Roscoe? He would be proud I know though he is long passed. Pace Roscoe Ripley does not sound so bad do you think? If it is a girl instead choose whatever name you want for a middle I do not care. Leaving it be is OK without a middle or you might want to put in your mother Marietta. Anyway is good. Just you stay healthy.

Your right this place is not so pretty as Pee Dee. Not pretty at all. There are boys inside these walls meaner than Peru you can bet. There is a Death House. I am getting along. The only thing is not thinking about the future. Your right there 10 years is not 2. The baby will be 10 but I will be 33. There is always a chance of early parole though the rap back home and the fact I busted parole there probably cancels that. I am not there idea of a good risk.

I really got no idea what happened to Perdita. She disappeared as you figured. She is a strange person and I did not know her well. Tell your mama I am dreadful sorry about each and everything that has happened and the last thing ever in my mind is to see you harmed. You are her daughter but I would like to marry you if you would consent while I am inside. This can be arranged because I asked. The preacher would do it but I know you cannot leave home. Maybe after you have the baby you would come here.

Write often peanut. I am in the laundry at 5. There are car magazines and TV. Other than that is mail.

I love you. It is hard to end this letter. If I stop writing your gone. There is not a lot more to say though. Vaya con dios mi amor.

Sailor

RITARDANDO

"I'm goin', Mama. No way I can't go."

"You ain't takin' Pace, though."

"Course I am, Mama."

Marietta sighed. "What time's Sailor's bus get in?"

"Six."

Neither Marietta nor Lula said anything for at least half a minute.

Finally, Marietta asked, "Got any plans?"

"Figure we'll go have supper someplace. Maybe get some barbecue out by Stateline. Sailor always liked that Havana Brown's Pig Pickin'."

"Well, you be careful with that boy, Lula."

"Sailor ain't a boy no more, Mama. He's thirty-three years old."

"Don't mean him," said Marietta. "It's Pace concerns me."

"Really, Mama, I gotta go."

"I'll be at Dal's, honey, you need me."

"Hi and all to Dal. We'll talk later."

"Bye, Lula. Love you."

"Love you."

Marietta hung up first. Lula was relieved that Marietta hadn't told her a second time to be careful.

"Pace? You ready, honey?"

The boy walked into the front room from the kitchen,

eating a chocolate bar. Lula got up from the couch and looked in the wall mirror.

"Shouldn't be eatin' no candy now, darlin'."

"Just a Mounds, Mama."

Lula finished fixing her hair, picked up her purse and headed for the door.

"Come, baby," she said.

From the back seat of the car, Pace said, "How'll we know what he looks like?"

Lula made a wide left turn onto Jeff Davis Highway without signaling, causing the driver of a white Thunderbird headed across the intersection to jam on his brakes in order to avoid a collision. The T-bird driver sat on his horn and shouted at Lula.

"Mama, you almost crashed us."

Lula steadied the steering wheel of her Camaro with her left elbow while she struck a match and lit up a More. She threw the match out the window and took possession of the wheel with both hands, the cigarette clamped in her teeth.

"Don't give me no trouble now, Pace, please. This ain't my easiest day in a long time. And what do you mean how we gonna know what your daddy looks like? You seen his photo."

"How'll he know what we look like? He seen our photo?"

Lula puffed furiously several times on her More before she took it out of her mouth and dropped it.

"Damn it, child! Now look what you made me do."

"What I make you do, Mama?"

Lula felt around on the floor with one hand until she found the cigarette.

"Nothin', honey," Lula said, stubbing it out in the ashtray. "Mama's just actin' strange."

"You ain't actin', Mama."

"Why, Pace Roscoe Ripley, ain't you got the cute mouth tonight."

"It's Grandmama does the actin'."

Lula didn't know whether to laugh or pretend to be angry.

"Who'd you hear that from?"

"Uncle Johnnie."

Lula laughed. "Then it must be true," she said.

"I still ain't sure what my daddy looks like."

"Like you, sweetheart. You and your daddy got the same mouth, eyes, ears and nose. Only difference is your color hair is black, like mine."

It started to rain, so Lula turned on the wipers, rolled up her window and flipped on the AC.

"My daddy ain't never killed nobody, has he, Mama?"

"Course he ain't never killed nobody. Why'd you say that, Pace?"

"Heard Uncle Johnnie and Grandmama talkin'."

"And?"

"Grandmama said how Sailor murdered a man."

"Wrong, baby. Your daddy never committed no murder. Musta been you didn't hear Grandmama proper. He made some mistakes, is all. Your daddy ain't always been so lucky."

Pace leaned over on the passenger side of the front seat and rolled down the window, letting the rain in.

"Pace, you close that. The seat's gettin' wet."

"I like the rain, Mama, it's steamin'."

Lula reached across and rolled the window back up.

"We're almost at the depot, honey. Sit back a minute."

Lula pulled the Camaro into a stall in the Trailways parking lot and cut the motor. She sat and watched as the blinking blue-and-white neon BUS sign gnawed its way through the grainy grey sky and sprawled across the windshield.

"Why we sittin' here, Mama?"

"Thinkin' a second, baby. Somethin' just now reminded me of a place me and your daddy stayed once."

"Where?"

"In a old hotel by the end of a river."

Lula shuddered and without thinking slid her right hand inside her shirt and caressed her left breast.

"Mama, it's hot."

Lula opened her door and she and Pace climbed out. They held hands as they walked through the warm rain toward the station. The big clock on the side of the building showed ten minutes past six.

"I'm scared, Mama."

"Why, honey?"

"Case Daddy don't like me. What if he don't like that I got black hair?"

"Pace, your daddy'd love you even if you didn't have no hair at all."

Lula saw Sailor as soon as she opened the door. He was sitting in an orange plastic chair against the opposite wall, smoking a cigarette.

"Still partial to Camels, huh?" Lula said to him.

Sailor smiled. "First pack of tailor-mades I had in a while," he said.

He stood up and looked down at Pace, who was still holding hands with Lula. Sailor put out his right hand.

"You must be my son," he said.

"Shake hands with your daddy," said Lula.

Pace released Lula's hand and put his own in Sailor's. Sailor gripped it gently but firmly, pumped once, then let go.

"Pleasure to meet you, Pace. I read a lot about you."

Sailor looked at Lula. Her eyes were full of tears and she let them loose.

"Good thing it's rainin'," she said, smiling. "Nobody'll know the difference."

"Nobody'd care but me," said Sailor.

Lula forced a laugh. "You hungry? Pace and I ain't had dinner yet."

"Lead the way."

Sailor picked up his black metal suitcase and followed them outside.

"No rag top, huh?" said Sailor as Lula drove.

Lula started to reply, then stopped. She stared straight ahead, gripping the wheel hard. Suddenly, she pulled over to the side of the road, killed the engine and got out of the car.

"What's wrong, Mama?" said Pace.

"Don't worry, son," Sailor said, turning to him and patting Pace's head. "Just stay here."

Sailor got out and went over to Lula, who was leaning back against the hood.

"I'm sorry, Sailor. I just can't help it. Give me a minute and I'll quit."

"Boy's frightened, Lula. This ain't no good."

"Really, Sail, I'll be okay. Look, it's just the rain now."

"It's a mistake, honey. You two go on. I'll walk back to the depot."

"What're you talkin' about? That's your son in there."

Sailor smiled. "He ain't never known me, Lula, so there ain't much for him to forget. Not seein' each other for ten years makes it next best to simple for us, too."

"How can you say that, Sailor?"

"What makes sense, is all."

Sailor went around to the driver's side, reached in and

pulled the keys out of the ignition. He unlocked the trunk, removed his suitcase and closed the lid.

"Don't do this, Sailor, please," said Lula.

Sailor slipped the keys in her shirt pocket and leaned his head into the car.

"*Oiga, amigo,*" he said to Pace. "If ever somethin' don't feel right to you, remember what Pancho said to the Cisco Kid: 'Let's went, before we are dancing at the end of a rope, without music.' "

Sailor stood up and looked at Lula. Her long black hair was matted from the rain and her eye makeup ran in dark streaks down her face.

"You been doin' fine without me, peanut. There ain't no need to make life tougher'n it has to be."

He picked up his suitcase, kissed Lula lightly on the lips and walked away. She let him go.

Barry Gifford was born in 1946 in Chicago, Illinois, and raised there and in Key West and Tampa, Florida. He is the author of the novels *Landscape with Traveler, Port Tropique,* and *An Unfortunate Woman,* several works of nonfiction, several volumes of poetry, and *The Devil Thumbs a Ride and Other Unforgettable Films,* a book of essays on film noir.

Mr. Gifford has received the Maxwell Perkins Award and a PEN Syndicated Fiction Prize, and was the founding editor of Black Lizard Books. He lives with his wife and two children in Berkeley, California.

VINTAGE
CONTEMPORARIES

VINTAGE CONTEMPORARIES

VINTAGE
CONTEMPORARIES

___ **California Bloodstock** by Terry McDonell	$8.95	679-72168-1
___ **The Bushwhacked Piano** by Thomas McGuane	$7.95	394-72642-1
___ **Keep the Change** by Thomas McGuane	$9.95	679-73033-8
___ **Nobody's Angel** by Thomas McGuane	$7.95	394-74738-0
___ **Something to Be Desired** by Thomas McGuane	$6.95	394-73156-5
___ **To Skin a Cat** by Thomas McGuane	$5.95	394-75521-9
___ **Bright Lights, Big City** by Jay McInerney	$5.95	394-72641-3
___ **Ransom** by Jay McInerney	$5.95	394-74118-8
___ **Story of My Life** by Jay McInerney	$6.95	679-72257-2
___ **Mama Day** by Gloria Naylor	$9.95	679-72181-9
___ **The All-Girl Football Team** by Lewis Nordan	$5.95	394-75701-7
___ **Welcome to the Arrow-Catcher Fair** by Lewis Nordan	$6.95	679-72164-9
___ **River Dogs** by Robert Olmstead	$6.95	394-74684-8
___ **Soft Water** by Robert Olmstead	$6.95	394-75752-1
___ **Family Resemblances** by Lowry Pei	$6.95	394-75528-6
___ **Sirens** by Steve Pett	$9.95	394-75712-2
___ **Clea & Zeus Divorce** by Emily Prager	$6.95	394-75591-X
___ **A Visit From the Footbinder** by Emily Prager	$6.95	394-75592-8
___ **Mohawk** by Richard Russo	$8.95	679-72577-6
___ **The Risk Pool** by Richard Russo	$8.95	679-72334-X
___ **Mile Zero** by Thomas Sanchez	$10.95	679-73260-8
___ **Rabbit Boss** by Thomas Sanchez	$8.95	679-72621-7
___ **Anywhere But Here** by Mona Simpson	$9.95	394-75559-6
___ **Carnival for the Gods** by Gladys Swan	$6.95	394-74330-X
___ **The Player** by Michael Tolkin	$7.95	679-72254-8
___ **Myra Breckinridge and Myron** by Gore Vidal	$8.95	394-75444-1
___ **All It Takes** by Patricia Volk	$8.95	679-73044-3
___ **The Car Thief** by Theodore Weesner	$6.95	394-74097-1
___ **Breaking and Entering** by Joy Williams	$6.95	394-75773-4
___ **Taking Care** by Joy Williams	$5.95	394-72912-9
___ **The Easter Parade** by Richard Yates	$8.95	679-72230-0
___ **Eleven Kinds of Loneliness** by Richard Yates	$8.95	679-72221-1
___ **Revolutionary Road** by Richard Yates	$8.95	679-72191-6

Now at your bookstore or call toll-free to order: 1-800-733-3000
(credit cards only).